ISSN: 2009-2369

The Linnet's Wings

I remain just one thing, and one thing only, and that is a clown.
It places me on a far higher plane than any politician.
Charlie Chaplin

The Linnet's Wings

AUTUMN 2014

Also by The Linnet's Wings:

The Song of Hiawatha by Henry Wadsworth Longfellow
One Day Tells its Tale to Another by Nonnie Augustine
Randolph Caldecott's The House that Jack Built

Frontispiece
A view of the artist's house and garden, in Mills Plains, Van Diemen's Land
  John Glover

TABLE OF CONTENTS
Autumn
Third Quarter 2014

ART

Managing Editor
Marie Fitzpatrick

Senior Editor
Bill West

Editors for Review
English
Bill West
Yvette Flis
Marie Fitzpatrick

Poetry
Oonah Joslin

Spanish
Marie Fitzpatrick

Contributing Editor
Martin Heavisides

Consulting on Photography
Maia Cavelli

Consulting on Copy
Digby Beaumont

Web and Database Management
Peter Gilkes

Websites Researched:
www.gutenberg.org/www. wikipaintings.org, www.goodreads.org

Don Quixote on Poetry

by

Miguel de Cervantes Saavedra

Girl Reading Book: Jose Ferraz de Almeida Junior

Poetry I regard as a tender virgin, young and extremely beautiful, whom divers other virgins—namely, all the other sciences—are assiduous to enrich, to polish, and adorn. She is to be served by them, and they are to be ennobled through her. But the same virgin is not to be rudely handled, nor dragged through the streets, nor exposed in the market-places, nor posted on the corners of gates of palaces. She is of so exquisite a nature that he who knows how to treat her will convert her into gold of the most inestimable value. He who possesses her should guard her with vigilance; neither suffering her to be polluted by obscene, nor degraded by dull and frivolous works. Although she must be in no wise venal, she is not, therefore, to despise the fair reward of honorable labors, either in heroic or dramatic composition. Buffoons must not come near her, neither must she be approached by the ignorant vulgar, who have no sense of her charms; and this term is equally applicable to all ranks, for whoever is ignorant is vulgar. He, therefore, who, with the qualifications I have named, devotes himself to poetry, will be honored and esteemed by all nations distinguished for intellectual cultivation.

Indeed, it is generally said that the gift of poesy is innate—that is, a poet is born a poet, and, thus endowed by Heaven, apparently without study or art, composes things which verify the saying, *Est Deus in nobis*, etc. Thus the poet of nature, who improves himself by art, rises far above him who is merely the creature of study. Art may improve, but cannot surpass nature; and, therefore, it is the union of both which produces the perfect poet.

Let him direct the shafts of satire against vice, in all its various forms, but not level them at individuals, like some who, rather than not indulge their mischievous wit, will hazard a disgraceful banishment to the Isles of Pontus. If the poet be correct in his morals, his verse will partake of the same purity: the pen is the tongue of the mind, and what his conceptions are, such will be his productions. The wise and virtuous subject who is gifted with a poetic genius is ever honored and enriched by his sovereign, and crowned with the leaves of the tree which the thunderbolt hurts not, as a token that all should respect those brows which are so honorably adorned

WIT AND WISDOM OF DON QUIXOTE

Editor's Note

I'm working late here and thinking about the social networks, but only because I've managed to lock myself out of my FB account, and because I can't get on to play it's made me reflect on the way in which our mind energies are gliding and connecting across the globe. Who knew even 5 years ago that so many cultures and social strata would open for perception to one and all and that we'd communicate openly with individuals without the addition of spin. To see and hear how others live in their reality without the input of the middle man: Broadsheet and TV news programmes. Once more we're hearing directly from the perosn on the street, the regular guy. It's great, and long may it last. With that in mind this poem caught my attention, it's from a book of poems by Bruce Harris, an English writer, who has contributed to 'The Linnet's Wing's' in past issues. It's from his new book 'Raised Voices,' which he released in September 2014.

Aliens coming to earth: Advice on timing by Bruce Harris

If you land in the fourteenth century, they'll probably think you're God
and, since you're all green and really quite small, they will tend to think it odd
that you haven't got beards or angel wings or arrive with a harp on a cloud;
you'll die of the Black Death anyway; they were quite an unhealthy crowd.

Fetching up in the sixteenth century, you'd be a religious plot;
they'd tie you and your ships to big wooden steaks and set fire to the whole damn lot;
anything made out of nice shiny cloth would be liable to requisition
and, if you do actually have little green balls, they'd be subject to Inquisition.

Coming down in the eighteenth century, you'll think them a bunch of prigs,
wafting white powder everywhere and poncing around in wigs.
You'll wonder about houses for coffee and bottles of gin everywhere;
mind, after one or two glasses of that you won't really bloody care.

Arriving in 1953, you'll need to be good at sports;
you'll need to play up and play the game and generally be good sorts.
Otherwise, you'll find yourself bent right over your spaceship bonnet
with your little green bottom up in the air and a thin cane descending upon it.

Opting for 1967 could well be a comfortable spot
though your little green kids will mumble about love and be going slowly to pot.

You'll wear ghastly kaftans and sit cross legged, with others of similar mind
and it won't be the wind between your ears which will slowly be blowing your mind.

Your landing in 1979 will be with a bump and a jerk;
they'll be jumping and bouncing around your ship and spitting on your paintwork.
Don't bother too much about dressing up and keep well away from the mobs;
they'll be desperate enough, in a very short time, to be pestering you for jobs.

Parking up in 1990, you'll need to watch how you go;
all the white powder lined up everywhere is not necessarily snow.
You'll be just in time to see La Thatcher succumb to the last attack
and, if you know which planet the woman is from, for pity's sake take her back.

And if you should choose to opt for now, our time has a lot to give
though you'll need to arrive with many green notes if you want to buy somewhere to live;
if no-one should turn up to meet your landing, don't worry, everything's fine,
it's just that no-one's interested much; we're all far too busy online.

…

    This quarter I'd like to welcome Oonah Joslin on board. She joined us for our Autumn issue to edit our poetry section, and I'm delighed to say she has agreed to stay awhile. We published Oonah's work in the past and she has been a contributing editor in some of our earlier issues.

    Many thanks to everyone involved in moving her out this quarter, most especially to our contributors who place their invaluable work in our hands for publication.

My best,

Marie

x

Sometimes I've believed as many as
six impossible things before breakfast.

Lewis Carrol

On with the Motley

by Oonah Joslin

Picture book for the niece of Ditha Mautner von Markhof

Artist: Koloman Moser

Tickle sat ring-side, chin on his fists and the corners of his mouth pulled down.

"What's up?" asked Tiny, sitting down beside him.

"I'm fed up," said the clown. "The circus is no fun, just work, work, work!"

"I know what you mean," sighed the elephant. "You rehearse and perform and the crowd goes wild; then you rehearse and perform again. Day in, day out, same old routine, except on travelling days and then it's *take the top down, put the top* up; up, down, up, down like a tart's..."

"And I mean, look at these huge feet!"

"I*'ve* got big feet," said Tiny, a little awkwardly.

"Yes, but you're a big animal; and you don't trip over yours. And then there's this enormous nose…"

Tiny squinted down at his own impressive proboscis. "Well, I can't of course agree with you…"

"Sorry, Tiny. No criticism intended. Anyway, yours isn't painted puce! And *you* get applause, whereas everybody just laughs at me."

"I just walk around the ring. It's *Julianne,* they applaud. I'm more like a big grey taxi, really. And grey… What kind of colour's grey for goodness sake? Look at you. You're bright and interesting to look at. You light up the ring. I don't do clever things like you do either. Even when I change direction I have to pretend it's because I'm afraid of a giant mouse. I'm not afraid of the stupid *mouse!*"

"Of course you're not," sympathised Tickle, who hadn't been able to get a word in all this time.

Pyro the dragon dropped in out of nowhere. I don't know why you *two* are moaning. Nobody even notices *me.*

"That's only because they can't see you, Pyro," said Tickle.

"What?"

"You're *mythical,* Pyro," added Tickle. "We've explained all this to you before." They explained it again.

Pyro looked downcast. But you *two* can see me.

"Yes, but that's because we believe in you."

"Why?"

"Well, because …" began Tiny, "because …"

Tickle stood up purposefully. "Because," he said, "friends believe in friends whether they're visible or not and that's what makes the whole freakin' circus work! Right?"

Previously published in The Pygmy Giant

The Whole Circus

Pyro the dragon flew around the big top trying to create a breeze, make the banners flap, make the canvas sides billow out ~ anything to get seen. He watched the audience applaud as Julianne somersaulted on Tiny's back. Tiny's huge feet plodded round the ring kicking up swirls of sawdust. He trumpeted with his long nose, knelt and stood and swished his little tail. They even went 'Oooooooo' when he did a huge poo ~ right there ~ on the circus floor. Tickle came with a bucket to scoop it up. Then he pretended to throw it at the crowd. The bucket had a false bottom of course.

'But at least they can see the bucket,' Pyro thought. 'It's not nice to be told that you're mythical ~ not even by friends. One wants to be a *little* mysterious of course but not totally invisible, not a complete *figment*.' And as he thought this, a tear trickled down to his nose and dripped onto the ring, unseen.

Tickle exited the ring, deliberately tripping over his feet and everybody cheered. A man dressed as a mouse ran in and Tiny, pretending to be startled,
raised his front legs so that Julianne could dismount and take her bow. Then he bowed too and lolloped out of the ring, chased by the arm-waving mouse.

As the audience dispersed, Pyro perched up on the high wire, watched disconsolate. 'Another show for them. Another no-show for me,' he thought. Just at that moment he lost his grip and plummeted. He spread his wings immediately of course but he also let out such a shriek of surprise that fire spurted from his nostrils and...and...

The people looked up. Some screamed. Some shouted, "What is that!?" "Oh the ugly thing!" Everybody ran. For just a moment Pyro was truly visible ~ a black little knobbly dragon silhouetted against the fire-light that was now consuming the Big Top.

It was headline news next day.
'Big Top Burns.'
'Mystery, Myth or Monster?'
'"Pyro-techics not part of Act,"' says Circus Owner.'

"Why did you do it?" asked Tickle kicking at a piece of scorched scenery with his shoe.

"I didn't mean to burn down the whole circus," Pyro said. "It just kind of happened."

"Well you certainly got noticed."

"But the people didn't like me. They were frightened of me." Pyro hung his large head and a black tear dropped onto Tiny's foot. "I've ruined everything."

"They'll put up another tent," Tiny said, withdrawing his foot from the danger of another scorching tear. "We'll paint new scenery. You can't help being a dragon, Pyro ~ no more than I have any choice about being an elephant," and he put a protective trunk around poor Pyro's scales.

"But Tickle had a choice about being a clown," said Pyro.

"Not so much as you'd think," said Tickle.

"What do you mean?" asked Pyro.

"You see, being a clown is more a question of choosing what people *don't* see than what they do see," said Tickle. "I allow you two to see me when I'm *not* being a clown but most people don't see me any more than they see you, Pyro ~ not the real me; or any more than they see Benny under his mouse costume."

"And I'm not afraid of the stupid mouse," interjected Tiny.

"Of course you're not," Tickle said. "You see, Pyro none of us is really real in public."

"Yes, I see that now," said Pyro. "Are you both very cross with me? Are we still friends?"

"Course we're friends!" said Tickle and Tiny both at once.

"Whether I'm visible or not...?" Pyro just thought he'd check.

"Hey!" said Tickle and he punched Pyro softly on his flank. "What I said before! The show must go on ~ remember?"

The Show Must Go On

"So ~ let me get this straight," Tickle was saying. "Julianne somersaults off your back onto my shoulders and then we tumble out of sight. Then Benny the mouse chases you once round the ring and exit ringside."

"Stupid mouse!" said Tiny.

"Okay, Tiny. We *know*. Now, do you want to rehearse?"

The rehearsal was flawless. The ringmaster was very pleased. Pyro sat up on the high-wire pedestal watching the new act and he cheered at the end. Of course only Tickle and Tiny heard this but they always appreciated his enthusiasm.

All went right on the first night until ~ out of nowhere a real mouse appeared and ran across Tiny's path. Julianne and Tickle tumbled out of the way just in time as Tiny turned tail, almost trampling Benny in his mouse suit and headed straight across the centre of the ring for the exit, at full pelt, leaving a very confused Benny, a furious ring master and a delighted audience laughing their heads off.

Tiny was in a lamentable state.

5

"So you're afraid of mice," said Pyro afterwards. "So what? I'm afraid of knights in armour. Everybody's afraid of something. Isn't that right, Tickle?"

"But now everybody knows the truth," said Tiny. "And they *laughed* at me."

"It's not so bad being laughed at. Isn't that right, Tickle? Better than frightening folk…" Pyro was trying really hard and he looked at Tickle in desperation wishing he'd chip in, or agree at least.

"Well, as you pointed out before, Pyro, I *chose* to be laughed at," said Tickle, "whereas Tiny here… Well he's just made a fool of himself in front of a large audience and he doesn't like that. I can see why he feels humiliated."

"Thanks a bunch!" said Tiny. "You clowns really know how to put the big boot in, don't you, Tickle. And I thought you were *my friend.*" The tip of Tiny's trunk was right down in the dirt and he looked greyer than the greyest grey ever.

"I *am* your friend," said Tickle "but there's not much point in friends lying to one another, Tiny. You feel humiliated. I'd feel just the same if I were you. But ~ be honest, we've always *known* this might happen."

"You have?" said Tiny.

"We've always known you were afraid of mice," said Pyro.

"How?" Tiny was genuinely astounded.

"Anyone," Tickle said, "who has to say 'I'm not afraid of the stupid mouse,' every day for this many years, has to be *terrified* of the things!"

For a grey animal, Tiny did a terrific pink blush.

"You know Pyro, sometimes friends need a little practical help," said Tickle folding his arms which he usually did when he was plotting something for the act. "Maybe there's a way to redress the balance?"

Tiny did his *running-away-from-the-mouse* act night after night without incident. His pusillanimous stampede out of the ring had actually increased ticket sales. Then one night, once again, a little mouse ran right out into the ring.

Julianne and Tickle tumbled out of the way just in time for Pyro to swoop from the high wire pedestal where he'd been keeping a look-out every night. Down in front of the elephant he dropped, prepared if necessary to scorch some dust.

"Who are you?" asked the startled mouse.

"A friend of Tiny's," said the dragon, pleased he could be seen, "and if you or any of your family try to embarrass my friend Tiny here again, I'm going to barbeque the lot of you and eat you like snacks. Got it?"

Small mammals are very perspicacious and this one thought retreat the better part of valour.

Of course nobody else could see Pyro, only Tiny who, quaking though he was, stood his ground so that to everyone in the crowd, it looked as if he was facing down the mouse, all by himself and when the terrified creature turned and ran across the sawdust, there rose a great round of applause and all the audience stood and cheered the elephant. Tiny winked at Pyro, drank in the accolade, trumpeted and took a bow.

Pyro took a deep bow too and though nobody other than Tickle and Tiny saw it, he was proud and content.

"Thanks," whispered Tiny.

"Bravo!" shouted Tickle from the side.

"The show must go on," said Pyro. "After all ~ that's what makes the whole freakin' circus work. Right?"

6 ###

Raised Voices

by

Bruce Harris

Do you like lyrical poems, ones that trap music within imagery? Do you like to read real poems? The ones that paint the reality of spin with a voice that can step outside ego, or the ones who just say it as it is now and describe how our reality was back 30/40 years ago when life was different. Or do you like your poetry to be fun, light and easy? Because whatever your preference is Bruce has it all covered in this collection. It's the type of work that a one can dip into for a lift, a smile, or a memory nudge or groan.

If you're like me you'll have a few favourite book of poems on the book shelf or maybe saved to a Kindle that you occasionally dip into. This is that type of book, I know I'll come back to 'Raised Voices' again for I was intrigued by the vision, as I saw circumstance evolve through the poet's eyes.

Here are small excerpts from a few of my favourites:

'Millie Elliot, Learning to Drill' The young ballet dancer who really wanted to become an engineer:

"Millie shouts out 'Mum, I'm home' and mutters 'at long last',
her leotard carelessly flung on the front hall easy chair.
One more day as a ballet girl has eventually and painfully past
and she can read again the mining books she keeps in her teenage lair.
A poster of a blasthole drill is secreted under her bed
and photos of heavy duty stopers hidden under her unitard;
her future is clear enough in her mind even though it's never been said
and isn't likely soon to be; all mining talk has been barred."

I wanted to paint the characters in 'The Day of the Dormouse.' I don't have room to show you why, so you'll have to take a read yourself ...

"Mad Hatters have days almost every other day,
on soap boxes, shouting, going on and on,
and no-one can doubt, in any possible way

the subjects that hatters have opinions on.
They're loud and expressive, with eloquence and brain,
but unhappily, straying quite close to insane."

and I thought about printing out out 'A Celebrity Virus' for a discussion opener in the pub, or as a lead in for some social comment in my art class group:

"Mothers, tensioned to weariest extremes,
just to hold back the humdrum day from anarchy;
fathers, rope-walking middle-aged bridges
over death chasms, leeched to bleeping machines;
youths, fresh dreams growing with limbs,
slapped savagely down by an angry reality;
girls, who have made themselves warm, misty places,
crushed that their beauty cannot be enough
and so, on it rumbles, the daily parade,
grotesque painted faces in tutored illusions
picking their gold from the back of the cash cows
even as they are mooing their soft adulations."

And there's more too. I know I wanted to slap the young lads that he portrayed in the 'Working Men's Club, Sunderland 1969.' And man his 'Seventies Staffroom' was depressing, but I've no doubt true; and then there's the sadness attached to lonely death which he pins. For there's a particular type of honesty trapped within each insightful thought that's driven by his choice of word, rhyme, and metaphor. It's a tip of a hat to a fine English voice that sees behind the fun, harshness and real living that hides within the day to day drama of living.

Bruce is also the editor of http://writingshortfiction.org , a free site offering advice, interactive questionnaires and resources for existing and aspiring short fiction writers. His book 'Raised Voices' can be bought from his own website: www.bruceharris.org

Marie Fitzpatrick

...

An Introduction to Participatory Democracy

and the New Irish Democratic Party

by

Ken Smollen

Since the onset of the recession in Ireland many people have questioned how and why a small group of people, banks and organisations could have brought our country and its people to our knees. Many people who ordinarily would not have had a huge interest in politics began to wonder if there was anything that could be done to alleviate the misery being imposed on our people by the present and last Governments. The severity and harshness of the austerity being imposed on people who were in no way responsible for the very questionable activities of banks, bond holders, large business and even our own Government led to many groups of people holding protests in many locations throughout the country.

However, it quickly became clear that protests alone would achieve very little as they were being totally ignored by the Government and they went largely unreported in the national media.

This then led to a number of meetings between people who were convinced that another way must be found to have the voices of ordinary people heard. In mid-October 2013, having studied different forms of Government throughout the world, a group of people emerged who were convinced that one particular system of governance definitely seemed to provide the fairness that has actually never before existed in Ireland. This system is called *Participatory Democracy*. It bears no resemblance whatsoever to the outdated and very corruptible *Representative Democracy* system that we have used since the foundation of the state.

Representative Democracy has existed for over 200 years. Its principles were deemed necessary at a time when the general population of the western world were largely uneducated with most people not being capable of making appropriate decisions that would best benefit the people in any of the countries in which it was practised! The answer to that was to allow the ordinary citizens to elect people of 'higher standing' who were deemed capable of making decisions on their behalf! Over the last number of decades it has become evident that *Representative Democracy* is very susceptible to corruption with the interests of banks, large businesses, multi-national corporations and very many lobby groups being placed before the interests of the very people it was originally designed to protect!

Despite the promises of many politicians past and present, what we experience at every election can be described as something similar to the children's game of musical chairs. Each Government consisting of elite representatives is replaced by another group of equally elite and privileged people who are cocooned and protected from the harshness of the life they impose on ordinary people!

Unbelievably this completely outdated system of democracy is still in use today. It is now so unfit for purpose that when the electorate vote at election time they are basically giving away their right to being involved in decisions that affect them. This realisation alone led to the birth of the **Irish Democratic Party** in late October 2013 in which we advocate a complete change in our system of governance to *Participatory Democracy.*

The principle of this system of democracy is that it is the electorate who have the final say in decisions being made that affect them. With the advancement of modern technology and with the use of social media and locally organised meetings, proposed decisions can now be discussed by the general population with the elected official's role being to vote in accordance with the majority of his/her electorate's decision. It also provides the safeguard that if any elected official fails to adhere to their electorates wishes they will be recalled and dismissed from their position. It also banishes the dreaded *'Whip'* system where at present elected representatives must vote in accordance with party leadership's wishes no matter what the consequences of such a decision for the people who elected them to their positions. *Participatory Democracy* will allow elected officials of the same party to vote in opposing ways in different constituencies, depending on how their own electorate want them to vote!

A very similar system of governance has existed in different parts of the world with great success. In the city of **Puerto Alegre** in **Brazil** the local population are allowed to participate in making decisions on how the local budget is spent. This has led to a far more equal and fair system and is called *Participatory Budgeting.* Following hurricane **Katrina** the people of **New Orleans** were also allowed to use this system where the local population could decide how best to spend the budget in order that they could repair their own city as they themselves saw fit. The famous author **George Orwell** spent some time in **Spain** during the **Spanish civil war** and in his book *'Homage to Catalonia'* he describes the use of *Participatory Democracy* which was used in parts of Spain during that time as the fairest form of democracy he had ever experienced!

The same system of governance which ensures fairness, equality, accountability and transparency can be tailor made to suit Ireland and our people and it's for that reason that our party was founded. The founding members of the **Irish Democratic Party** were **Ken Smollen, William Bryan** and **Edward Lennon.** We were quickly joined by **Laura Smollen** and **Angela Briggs.** These five people are deemed to be the original founding/executive committee of the **IDP** whose role it is to steer the party in the direction for which it was founded. **Ken Smollen** is a former Garda having been stationed in **Tallaght, Edenderry** and **Portlaoise** before retiring after 30 years' service. **William Bryan** is a Disability Transport Provider and is based in **Geashill, Co. Offaly. Edward Lennon** is a taxi driver from **Tullamore, Co. Offaly. Laura Smollen** is a Registered General Nurse in **Tullamore General Hospital. Angela Briggs** is a housewife and carer for her youngest daughter.

The commitment required in founding and running a new political party is immense and is aided by the fact that all of the present Executive Committee live close to Tullamore where we meet twice every week in the run up to the official launch of the Irish Democratic Party which takes place in the Bridge House Hotel, Tullamore, Co. Offaly on Saturday 25th October.

This event will create political history for three reasons: -

1: It is the first time that a political party has been launched in Tullamore since the foundation of the state

2: The **IDP** is the first party in Ireland to advocate a complete change in the political system that's used in Ireland, namely the change to *'Participatory Democracy'*

3: And every member of the **IDP** is an ordinary person with experience of the hardship that elite groups of elected representatives have imposed on our people.

We don't have any former or ex-politicians on board and neither will we allow our party to be used by former politicians to revive their careers!

One of the first objectives that we now have is to gain the attention of the media both locally, nationally and even internationally. The first article that was written about the IDP appeared in the **Offaly Independent** about two months ago. The second article appeared in the **Tullamore Tribune** on 4th September with the headline, *'Political History To Be Made In Tullamore'*.

The **Irish Democratic Party** can rightly claim to be totally unique in Ireland in that we are the only political party in the country that offers our people the only real and genuine alternative to what they have experienced since our state was founded. Every other party and all Independents are content to use the *Representative Democracy* system of governance which has served our people so badly for decades, whereas the IDP advocates a complete change from this clearly outdated and very corruptible system to the much fairer system of *Participatory Democracy*!

To date we have members in twenty two counties in the country. We also have members in *N. Ireland, England, France, Bulgaria, USA, Canada*, and as far away as *Cambodia*. All of this has been achieved via social media and without any funding or the use of any printed material whatsoever. We now have our website up and running. This can be seen at *www.IrishDemocraticParty.ie.* Very shortly we will have our very first leaflets printed which will explain exactly who we are and what the **IDP** is all about.

As previously stated, the official launch of Ireland's newest political party will take place, on Saturday 25th October, in **The Bridge House Hotel, Tullamore** from 2 – 4pm, and everyone is more than welcome to attend what will surely be the opening of a completely new chapter in the history of Ireland and our people.

...

QUOTES

I am a firm believer in the people. If given the truth, they can be depended upon to meet any national crisis. The great point is to bring them the real facts, and beer.

Abraham Lincoln

Democracy works when people claim it as their own.

BILL MOYERS, The Nation, Jan. 22, 200

The first duty of a man is to think for himself

José Martí

The strongest democracies flourish from frequent and lively debate, but they endure when people of every background and belief find a way to set aside smaller differences in service of a greater purpose.

BARACK OBAMA, press conference, Feb. 9, 2009

The death of democracy is not likely to be an assassination from ambush. It will be a slow extinction from apathy, indifference, and undernourishment.

ROBERT HUTCHINS

Modern democracies will face difficult new challenges--fighting terrorism, adjusting to globalization, adapting to an aging society--and they will have to make their system work much better than it currently does. That means making democratic decision-making effective, reintegrating constitutional liberalism into the practice of democracy, rebuilding broken political institutions and civic associations. Perhaps most difficult of all, it requires that those with immense power in our societies embrace their responsibilities, lead, and set standards that are not only legal, but moral. Without this inner stuffing, democracy will become an empty shell, not simply inadequate but potentially dangerous, bringing with it the erosion of liberty, the manipulation of freedom, and the decay of a common life.

FAREED ZAKARIA, The Future of Freedom

Democracy is when the indigent, and not the men of property, are the rulers.

ARISTOTLE

Churchyard at Shillingstone by Tom Roberts

ELEGY

WRITTEN IN A COUNTRY CHURCHYARD

Thomas Gray

The curfew tolls the knell of parting day,
  The lowing herd wind slowly o'er the lea,
The plowman homeward plods his weary way,
  And leaves the world to darkness and to me.

Now fades the glimmering landscape on the sight,
  And all the air a solemn stillness holds,
Save where the beetle wheels his droning flight,
  And drowsy tinklings lull the distant folds:

Save that, from yonder ivy-mantled tower,
  The moping owl does to the moon complain
Of such as, wandering near her secret bower,
  Molest her ancient solitary reign.

TRADUCCION DE LA ELEGIA
Escrita por Gray en el cementerio de una iglesia de aldea.

El toque de queda sonidos el tañido de la muriendo día;
La manada mugido se muden lento sobre la colina,
El regreso a casa labrador plods su fatigoso camino
Y deja el mundo a la oscuridad y me.

Ahora se desvanece el paisaje que brilla tenuemente en la
  vista,
Y todo el aire una quietud solemne sostenga,
Hasta que el escarabajo gire su zángano vuelo
Y el suave tintineo soñolientos arrullen los pliegues distantes;

Hasta que desde allá torre hiedra de manto
Un moping búho haga a la luna se queja
De tal como, vagando cerca ella secreto enramada
Moleste su antiguo reinado solitario.

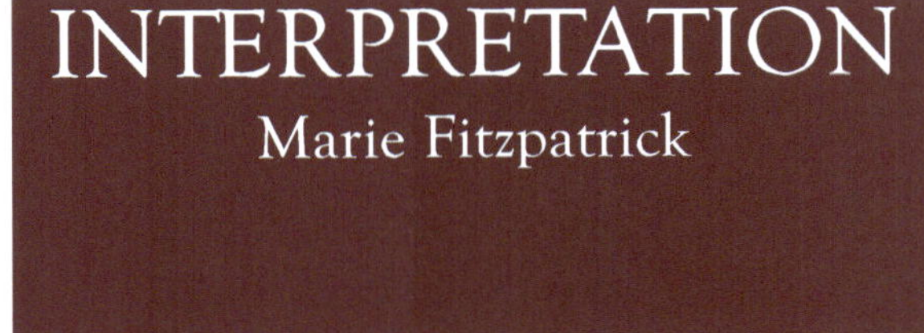

Beneath those rugged elms, that yew-tree's shade,
　　Where heaves the turf in many a mouldering heap,
Each in his narrow cell forever laid,
　　The rude forefathers of the hamlet sleep.

The breezy call of incense-breathing morn,
　　The swallow twittering from the straw-built shed,
The cock's shrill clarion, or the echoing horn,
　　No more shall rouse them from their lowly bed

For them no more the blazing hearth shall burn,
　　Or busy housewife ply her evening care;
No children run to lisp their sire's return,
　　Or climb his knees the envied kiss to share

Oft did the harvest to their sickle yield,
　　Their furrow oft the stubborn glebe has broke;
How jocund did they drive their team afield!
　　How bow'd the woods beneath their sturdy stroke!

Let not Ambition mock their useful toil,
　　Their homely joys, and destiny obscure;
Nor Grandeur hear with a disdainful smile
　　The short and simple annals of the poor

Debajo de esos olmos robustos, que sombra de tejo árbol,
Donde palpite el césped en muchos un montón mouldering,
Cada uno en su estrecha celda para siempre tumbado,
El grosero antepasados del caserío el sueño.

La llamada brisa de la mañana incienso-respiración,
La golondrina twitteando desde el cobertizo de paja construida,
Clarín estridente del gallo, o el cuerno resonando,
Nunca más volverá se despierten de su cama humilde.

Para ellos no es más la chimenea ardiente quemarán,
O ama de casa ocupada surcan su cuidado de noche;
No hay niños corran a balbucear el regreso de su padre,
O suba sus rodillas el beso envidiado compartir.

A menudo lo hizo, la cosecha a sus hoz cedan
Su surco oft la gleba terca ha roto;
¡Cómo jocund hagan que conducen a su equipo lejos!!
¡Cómose se marchiten los bosques de bajo de su golpe robusto!

Que no Ambition burlan su esfuerzo útil,
Sus acogedoras alegrías y oscuro destino,
Ni grandeza escuche con una sonrisa desdeñosa,,
Los anales cortos y sencillos de los pobres.

The boast of heraldry, the pomp of power,
   And all that beauty, all that wealth e'er gave,
Awaits alike th' inevitable hour.
   The paths of glory lead but to the grave.

Nor you, ye proud, impute to these the fault,
   If Memory o'er their tomb no trophies raise;
Where, through the long-drawn aisle and fretted vault,
   The pealing anthem swells the note of praise.

Can storied urn or animated bust
   Back to its mansion call the fleeting breath?
Can Honour's voice provoke the silent dust?
   Or Flattery soothe the dull cold ear of Death?

Perhaps in this neglected spot is laid
   Some heart once pregnant with celestial fire;
Hands, that the rod of empire might have sway'd,
   Or wak'd to ecstasy the living lyre:

But Knowledge to their eyes her ample page,
   Rich with the spoils of time, did ne'er unroll;
Chill Penury repress'd their noble rage,
   And froze the genial current of the soul.

El alarde de la heráldica, la pompa del poder
Y toda esa belleza, toda esa riqueza nunca dio,
Espera por igual el hora inevitable,
La senda de la gloria va al sepulcro.

Ni vosotros, orgulloso, imputa a éstos el culpa,
Si memoria sobre su tumba no trofeos levantan;
Donde, a través del largo-pasillo y repujado bóveda,
El himno pealing aumente la nota de elogio.

Puede urna estratificada o busto animado
¡Mientras atrás en a su mansión el llamada el fugaz aliento?
¿ Puede voz de honor provoque el polvo silencioso?
¿O adulación a calme el oído sordo frío de la muerte?

Tal vez en este lugar descuidado esté asinge,
Un corazón una vez embarazada con fuego celestial;
Las Manos, que la varilla del imperio pudo haber influido,
O despertado al éxtasis la lira viviente.

Pero el conocimiento de sus ojos la amplia página,
Ricos con los botines de tiempo, nunca no hizo desenrollar
Chill Penury reprimió su rabia noble,
Y se congeló la corriente genial del alma.

Full many a gem of purest ray serene
    The dark unfathom'd caves of ocean bear;
Full many a flower is born to blush unseen,
    And waste its sweetness on the desert air.

Some village Hampden, that with dauntless breast
    The little tyrant of his fields withstood,
Some mute inglorious Milton here may rest,
    Some Cromwell, guiltless of his country's blood.

Th' applause of listening senates to command,
    The threats of pain and ruin to despise,
To scatter plenty o'er a smiling land,
    And read their history in a nation's eyes,

Their lot forbade: nor circumscrib'd alone
    Their growing virtues, but their crimes confin'd;
Forbade to wade through slaughter to a throne,
    And shut the gates of mercy on mankind,

The struggling pangs of conscious truth to hide,
    To quench the blushes of ingenuous shame,
Or heap the shrine of Luxury and Pride
    With incense kindled at the Muse's flame.

Lleno muchos una joya de rayo más puro sereno,
Las cuevas insondables oscuras el mar lleven:
Lleno muchas flores nace a ruborizarse invisible,
Y gaste su dulzura en el aire del desierto.

Algún pueblo Hampden, ése con pecho dauntless,
El pequeño tirano de sus campos resistido,
Algunos mudo ignominioso Milton aquí puede descanse,
Algunos Cromwell, inocente de la sangre de su país

El aplauso de escuchando senados al mando,
Las amenazas de dolor y ruina despreciar,
Para esparcir abundancia sobre una tierra sonriente,
Y leer su historia en los ojos de una nación,

Su suerte prohibió: ni circunscrito solo
Sus virtudes crecimiento, pero su crímenes confinado;
Prohibido que vadear a través de masacrea el trono,
Y lo cierran ellos puertas de la misericordia a la humanidad,

Los tormentos de lucha de verdad conscienteesto esconde,
Sofocar el rubor de vergüenza ingenua,
O montón el Santuario de lujo y orgullo,
Con incienso encendido en llamas de la musa.

Far from the madding crowd's ignoble strife,
    Their sober wishes never learn'd to stray;
Along the cool sequester'd vale of life
    They kept the noiseless tenor of their way.

Yet even these bones from insult to protect,
    Some frail memorial still erected nigh,
With uncouth rhymes and shapeless sculpture deck'd,
    Implores the passing tribute of a sigh.

Their name, their years, spelt by th' unletter'd Muse,
    The place of fame and elegy supply;
And many a holy text around she strews,
    That teach the rustic moralist to die.

For who, to dumb forgetfulness a prey,
    This pleasing anxious being e'er resign'd,
Left the warm precincts of the cheerful day,
    Nor cast one longing lingering look behind?

On some fond breast the parting soul relies,
    Some pious drops the closing eye requires;
Even from the tomb the voice of Nature cries,
    Even in our ashes live their wonted fires.

Lejos de lucha innoble del mundanal conflictos,
Sus deseos sobrios nunca aprendido se desvíen;
A lo largo del valle secuestrado fresco de la vida
Mantuvieron el tenor silencioso de su inclinación.

Pero incluso estos huesos de insultoa proteger,
Un frágil memorial aún erigido cerca,
Con rimas zafios y escultura sin forma engalanado,
Implora el tributo de pasar de una suspiro.

Sus nombre, sus años, deletreó por la musa iletrada,
El lugar de la fama y elegía provee
Y muchos un texto sagrado, alrededor, ella esparce
Que ensenar la rústica moralista morir.

Por quien a olvido estúpido una víctima,
Este agradable preocupada siendo alguna vez reconciliado
Dejó el cálido recintos del día alegre
Ni eche un anhelo persistente mirada atrás?

En algunos aficionado a pecho el alma dejando confíe,
Algunas gotas piadosas que el ojo cierre requiere,
Incluso desde la tumba, la voz de la Naturaleza grite,
Incluso en nuestras cenizas vivir sus usual incendios.

For thee, who, mindful of th' unhonour'd dead,
   Dost in these lines their artless tale relate,
If chance, by lonely contemplation led,
   Some kindred spirit shall inquire thy fate,

Haply some hoary-headed swain may say,
   "Oft have we seen him at the peep of dawn
Brushing with hasty steps the dews away,
   To meet the sun upon the upland lawn.

"There at the foot of yonder nodding beech,
   That wreathes its old fantastic roots so high,
His listless length at noontide would he stretch,
   And pore upon the brook that babbles by.

"Hard by yon wood, now smiling as in scorn,
   Muttering his wayward fancies he would rove;
Now drooping, woeful-wan, like one forlorn,
   Or craz'd with care, or cross'd in hopeless love.

"One morn I miss'd him on the custom'd hill,
   Along the heath, and near his favourite tree;
Another came; nor yet beside the rill,
   Nor up the lawn, nor at the wood was he;

"The next, with dirges due in sad array,
   Slow through the church-way path we saw him borne.
Approach and read (for thou canst read) the lay
   Grav'd on the stone beneath yon aged thorn."

Para ustedes que son pensando de el humilde muertos.
En estas líneas su historia ingenua relacionan;
Si azar, por contemplación sola dirigió,
Algunos espíritu afín inquirierede tu destino,

Tal vez un viejo admirador se puede decir,
"A menudo hemos visto al amanecer
Barriendo el rocío estar lejos con rápido pasos,
A encontrar el sol sobre el césped tierra alta."

Allí, a los pies la haya asintiendo allá
Que coronas su antiguo fantástico raíces tan alto,,
'Su longitud apático al mediodía el iría a estirar,
Y que contemplaría el riachuelo que murmura por.

Cerca de la bosque, ahora sonrisa, como en desprecio,
Mascullando su obstinado fantasías el iría,
Ahora caídos, lamentable-wan, como uno abandonado,
O enloquecidos con cuidado, o cruzado en amor sin
   esperanza.

Uno mañana, yo lo extrañaba sobre la colina habitual,
A lo largo del pástar y cerca de su árbol favorito;
Otro vino; ni todavía cerca de el riachuelo
Ni en el césped, ni en la madera era él;

'El siguiente, con cantos fúnebres debido en triste array
'lento a través de la iglesia-way camino que lo vimos
   transmitidas;
Enfoque y leer, (para usted que sabe como leer,) el epitafio
Escrito en el piedra debajó el anciano árbol"

The Epitaph

Here rests his head upon the lap of earth
A youth to fortune and to fame unknown:
Fair Science frown'd not on his humble birth,
And Melancholy marked him for her own.

Large was his bount}', and his soul sincere,
Heaven did a recompense as largely send:
He gave to mis'ry (all he had) a tear,
He gained from heav'n ('t was all he wished) a friend.

No farther seek his merits to disclose,
Or draw his frailties from their dread abode
(There they alike in trembling hope repose),
The bosom of his Father and his God.

El Epitafio

Aquí, descansa su cabeza sobre la regazo de la tierra
Una juventud a fortuna y a fama desconocida
Feria ciencia no frunce en su nacimiento humilde.
Y tristeza lo marcó para su propio

Grande fue su generosidad y su alma sincera,
El cielo hizo una recompensa como enviar en gran medida:,
Le dio a la miseria, todo lo que tenía, una lágrima
Obtuvo del cielo ('twas todo lo que deseaba) un amigo.

No más lejos busque sus méritos revelar,
O dibujar sus flaquezas de su temible morada,
Allí son iguales en esperanza temblorosa reposan,
El seno de su padre y su Dios.

Knotted Fables

Novella Excerpt

by

John P. Bourgeois

Based on how frequently she saw the stork and heard the bird's clacking beak, the hare knew she was kilometers ahead of the tortoise. Comforted by this, she stopped to graze at a particularly emerald patch of nettles and dandelions. The run had famished her, but the hare did not want to eat her fill at the banquet. Not in front of the other animals.

"The victor must be genteel," she told herself.

The hare ate. The afternoon sun wallowed in the soft light on her calico coat and in the brilliancy of the tender leaves. The hare thought about how she had arrived at this life juncture.

"What am I doing in this race? If I win, I look like a bully. If I lose, I look like a liar and a slowpoke, slower than a tortoise! If only I'd kept my mouth shut…nothing gained, all lost. The tortoise *did* insult me! But only after I made fun of him."

The hare nibbled on another rumination.

"Will a lion be at the feast? Did the fox invite lions? Or wolves? Great. Win or lose, I still lose. Why go on? Maybe if I'd thought, I could stay here and munch quietly in this lovely spot."

She did just that, for a moment.

"Can I quit the race? How would that look?! Not any worse than finishing as dinner at my own banquet." Her stressing had destroyed her appetite, but she tarried in the meadow. When the stork came again, the hare concealed herself beneath a rhododendron. The tortoise passed his adversary's idyllic refuge. The hare still hid.

She was oblivious to the lion stalking out of the forest's undergrowth.

In the same woods but at a different time, the hare had rejoiced. Yet, her jubilation ruined the spring poetry by injecting raucousness into the drone of the thawing forest. The hare bragged about her latest exploit to all, both those who would willingly listen and most trying to escape the racket. Hopping ecstatically, almost frenetically, evangelically, so that even the aloof ravens above the canopy heard, the hare thumped on the fresh grass to signal that all of creation's attention belonged to her.

"I'm so fast even the lion can't catch me! He tried! Yes, did he try!" her tale began again. "I was like zoom, vroom, KABOOM! That last bit, that 'kaboom,' that's where I kicked a sandstorm worth of dust right in his open mouth. And right too when he thought he had me!”

The claims echoed throughout the woods, woods where only minutes prior larks had garbled their syrupy woos; shabby squirrels had stored fur coats for next autumn; and itching twigs eased forth leaf buds in the same manner that one might imagine growing fingernails. Although the place had not been quiet, its tone had been more measured, the meter more regular. Now, harmony had not only left, it had left no vestiges of its having been there.

“Big, ole lion coughing and hacking while I hippity-hopped away.”

The hare reenacted the scene. The danger's seriousness lost its bite as the herbivorous-bucked teeth gaped in no semblance of ferocity, let alone abject terror. This poor showing drew giggles from the captive (not captivated) audience, laughter the hare saw as approval.

“Easy as air I was. He had nothing! Nothing! Nada on me!”

After the first recitation, animals had applauded politely. Since the encore performances signaled no reprieve, the claps had subsided into bored silence that lasted for a half-minute before the hare restarted. The story amused none any longer, yet none resumed their own business. All were the hare's prisoners. Her monotony incarcerated them.

Velveteen paws gestured grandiosely. With only minor variations, the hare harangued the woods until she annoyed the trees themselves, to mention nothing of their suffering inhabitants. She bound from boulder to birch, from beech to brook in case any living creature hoped to evade her story. The hare raconteured ad nauseum to the whole forest.

A dry winter had left two months prior, and the encroaching summer looked to be a sticky scorcher. This middle season was a respite from extremes. In its moderation though, spring became an exaggeration of normality. The relative climatic calm allowed life to awaken from its deep frozen nap. Or perhaps life had not even slept but merely been forgotten? For its part, maybe spring too had merely been remembered, never having slept or even left? Could it be possible that the very act of anthropomorphizing nature diminishes its innate beauty by reconstructing it as somehow human?

It is best not ponder such digressions here.

The blowhard hare broke all tranquility, innate or introduced. Unable to get away from this ego-bloated mammal, one animal opined an alternate perspective on the reported event.

“You are telling us that you almost got caught, then?” the tortoise asked after twenty minutes of trying to outpace the hare and another five of trying to ignore the story. Dry amusement puckered his face. His eyes criticized the hubris in leporiform.

An interruption to her narrative did not long befuddle the hare.

"Shoot, almost got caught! That's what you think and what the lion thought, but that's not how it went! Now, you, little tortoise man, you wouldn't have had a chance – big cat versus little you."

"Is that so?"

The baseless braggart irked the normally patient tortoise. He attempted to burrow but could not penetrate the parched soil. The hyped-up hare persisted her assault. The tortoise thought slowly yet deeply and could not have kept pace with the hare attack. Instead of composing retorts that he could not deliver until they were too old to have any bite, he dedicated his energies to munching on violets. The flower scented his shearing beak. He would have liked to have lingered in the odor. That clean, purple odor. Any activity, any sense to distract him from the hare.

For her part, the hare mistook the tortoise's silence as smugness.

"What?! You, you think you could have outrun the lion? With your stubby turtle feet and scaly legs?!"

She jumped in circles around him. She crushed the flowers, and their bruised petals scented the air that vibrated with the hare-sterical abuse. The taciturn stoic stood his ground. Tension built between the dynamic and static. The probability of collision fattened in the void and grew unavoidable. The force that had enjoined the forest to listen to the hare's story now enjoined it to listen to her attack. Animals are said to sense nearing storms.

"Plus, did you know you have an RV hitched to you? What is that on your top, a pueblo?" She rapped on the shell, "Hello, anyone home? 'Just us lion food.'"

The hare hunched onto all fours and drew her face taut to taunt the tortoise's attenuated features while impersonating his morose timbre. She had the impertinence to eat the last unblemished violet.

As the hare continued to billow the tortoise's boiling temper, the crowd of animals swelled. They were eager to hear news other than the hare's boasts, and the tortoise had been haughty to each of them at least once, or so every observer had imagined. Egged on by the audience's renewed attention, the hare bounced atop the reptile's shell, onto his feet, near his bald head. During this torrent of motion, the hare continuously insulted the tortoise on the full catalog of unfathomable topics. Most are unprintable here.

Without escape, the tortoise lost himself in muzzled fury. Even the messianic calm will flip a table when pushed. How the tortoise had been pushed! Bright shapes popped before his withered face. His stomach knotted. His three chambered heart raced like it had seven. Time dilated. The cruelty went on and on and on, as old and vain as spring itself. Finally, the tortoise exploded.

"Look, Fuzzy!" he snapped, "If you are so sure that you can beat me - shell and all- how about a race?"

Cocking his head at an angle so extreme that he could have cricked his own neck, the tortoise narrowed his garrulous eyes. Though the tortoise's initial comment had not flustered her, the hare scratched her head at this proposal.

"Well, I don't know...I mean..." She looked at the crowd, which looked back at her. The hare would have wished the other animals gone now, now that she appeared to be a warmonger rather than a comedienne.

The tortoise saw his enemy's turmoil. Reason had passed from him. Escape and dignity had fled both adversaries, leaving them bare to the observers' ravenous, crazed, hungry stares. Again, the tortoise pressed.

"Are you afraid? If you won't face a slow tortoise, how do we know that there ever was a lion, or is it some fur-brained story?" The tortoise imitated the hare, "'I beat a lion, yes I did. Beat him good like a rug. Beat him like a meringue.'"

"You really expect to win?" she asked in voice lowered so as to hopefully not be heard by the other animals.

The tortoise guffawed, "You are afraid! I did not think you could act like such a mouse. This makes me wonder how much of your reputation has been embellished." The tortoise got right in the hare's reddening face to accuse her. "I bet you don't even like carrots."

The crowd gasped.

This insult set any caution in the hare's heart afire. Its ashes left only vindication. She crossed her arms over her chest in resolution and found her original swagger once more.

"Fine, lil' tortoise man. We'll have your silly race. And when I win, we'll have a big party compliments of the loser to celebrate me conquering the lion and whipping you with these big, beautiful feet."

Emboldened, she kissed each of her soles, as a boxer might kiss flexed biceps in intimidation. The tortoise only nodded and leered. A smudge of the hare's foot grit had dirtied her nose.

With the braggadocio of the hare, the spunk of the tortoise, and the guarantee of a party after the race, multitudes assembled two weeks later. A dog took wagers. Despite the banquet to follow, vendors sold concessions. Organic grub juice washed down currant cakes, mulberry mochi, and kudzu puddings. Modifying his plans, the fox did not festoon the race grounds in streamers and lanterns due to the risk of rain. Grasshoppers played their frivolous madrigals and courageous ballads on woodwind, percussion, and strings. Several of the insects even sang traveling songs about waltzing Maddie. The other animals secretly jigged to the music, tapping their toes as they strode past. However, if they stood nearby to listen, the grasshoppers would demand to be paid and harass the listeners.

"Pay if you enjoy it," the grasshoppers chirped.

In coughed excuses, the patrons dispersed.

A stork stretched her wings and performed vocal exercises. Her otherwise meager voice resonated through her megaphone of a beak. She would provide the commentary, flying between the runners and the information-eager crowd. From her bill clattered an arpeggio, until she heard what a failure the exercise was and switched to tongue twisters.

She repeated ever faster, "Wisp wrists wither water while wings wattle wrangling rung."

At the starting line, the tortoise and the hare psyched up themselves while psyching out their opponent. The hare did jumping jacks. Her ears drummed against the tortoise's shell in a petty effort to annoy the reptile. For his part, the tortoise did not prepare in any way other than extending each appendage (neck, arms, legs, tail) in turn as far as possible and waving said appendage around. From far away, the maneuver looked like a ridiculous dance. The other animals watched curiously eager for the race.

The scents of feasting had lured a soldier ant who escorted seven workers for derelict scraps. At the race grounds, the insects searched among the spectators' feet.

"What a way to spend a day," exhorted the soldier.

"Better than foraging," replied one of a nearby grasshopper quartet.

"We'll see," the soldier scoffed with a shrug.

From beneath a food cart, two half-buried frogs watched this chatter but spoke only to each other. They murmured softly, but even in their quietness, mud and fear's sallowness subdued their tone.

In spite of the convivial banter and splendor around them, to the competitors this race was very serious, very expensive business.

"You ready to pay? I'm feeling a shy peckish. You'll need half dozen banquets just for me."

"First, you have to win, and I've been practicing," the tortoise lied. He lowered his racing goggles. The hare threw an aviator's scarf jauntily over her shoulder. The stork flew to the starting line. A clover chain stretched between two trees. She stood in the middle of the lane and cast the most minuscule shadow in the late morning. After having given instructions to the racers, the stork sounded for general silence. Opening remarks outlined the day's schedule, the course, the fete to follow. Occasionally the stork tilted her head upward to try to remember an obscure detail. Hearing the restless crowd shifting, she forewent the minutiae and hastened to start.

"Mark.

Set.

GO!"

The stork snipped the florid link with a beak's clap. The scarf whipped the air. Dust billowed from the line. The hare dashed like a hyphen. When the dirt cloud settled, the tortoise had not moved his entire body beyond his starting position. After cheering for the ribbon cutting, the animals looked pitifully at the racing reptile then dubiously at each other. The outcome seemed foregone. They all marveled at the contest's futility.

Well most marveled anyway. Busy overseeing the exactness of his caterers' preparations, the fox would not have known that the race started had it not been for the mass's cacophony. "So much to do," he moaned. "I hope they don't finish the race for at least an eon, preferably two."

He seemed to get his wish. Hours passed with nary a sign of the competitors. Well, the tortoise remained in sight half an hour after the hare had disappeared. When the racers had gone, the stork flew from the hare to the tortoise and back to the party with progress updates. By the time she delivered these reports, both contestants had traveled farther apart and farther along the course. Exact locations were never known. Besides, the hare would surely win. With every update, the absurdity of the competition became more obvious. Four miles apart, ten miles, then fifteen. The hare passed the halfway marker before the tortoise had traveled even a quarter of the way. Among timber and over meadows, the solo animals went. As the race was run, tempers lessened. The hare tired. She stopped to rest and reflect in an especially verdant spot.

"I lost her," the stork admitted.

Truth be told, the stork had not seen the hare in more than an hour but had kept searching. The bird needed to find the mammal. Hopelessly, she returned to the spectators to face her rebuke.

"What do you mean? How'd that happen? Silly bird!" The animals churned.

The vendors' stocks had been depleted, and the fox would not allow the crowd to have only a soupçon of the upcoming feast. The multitudes were hungry and restless. Hangrily, they considered eating the useless stork.

"The tortoise is about halfway through. I'll go look for the hare some more."

Harsh words trailing her, the stork rushed to find the anticipated winner.

Like a mirage in the wavering heat of late afternoon, the lethargic throng saw the myopic tortoise before he could see them. Encouraging him to hurry, the animals cheered. The loudest were those who bet on him; the tortoise paid 9 to 1. The dog looked forlorn and annulled all his bets.

Not one to be bandwagon inveigled, the tortoise kept his pace and was,

slowly,

   inexorably,

      finally

TRIUMPHANT!

Cymbals clanged as he crossed the finish line. The result was unexpected. A fluke. No one foresaw it.

"Where's the hare?" the tortoise asked once he had caught his breath.

"No one's seen her," said the grumpy dog.

"Probably preoccupied by her reflection, the vain rodent!"

The tortoise had never won anything before and did not know how to comport himself. "Am I the greatest creature alive?" he asked himself. Conquest empowered him. "How can I feel so good!?"

The stork placed a laurel on the tortoise's head, but it slid down to become a leafy necklace instead.

The animals feasted, guffawed, and gallivanted for hours, for days. Struggling to keep up, the fox's servers circulated around with berry kabobs and fruity drinks. Romaine wraps went rapidly. On spits, sheep-laden rotisseries rotated under the carnivores' drooling eyes. The fire lighted the revelry until the sun rose again, and the animals cavorted into the next day without notice or shame. During that time, the other animals berated the stork for losing the hare who had still not arrived. The stork did not mind in the slightest and hooted with the others, stumbling over her own lanky legs when they got tied up in her beak. This balance problem of hers did not improve as the party wore on.

On the other hand, the tortoise watched from his place of honor on the dais. He nibbled on minced horn melon and declined repeated offers to soak his achy legs in scalding mud baths. With disgruntled biliousness, the tortoise lorded over the crowd. His win was nothing if the hare were not there.

Two

On the second day, the dog left the party. His distended abdomen almost scraped the ground. Sticky drinks and fat drippings splotched his brindle coat. Happily for him and his narcissism, the sun's brilliance perforating the conifers dappled the pine strewn floor. Mottled coolness covered his stained fur. In spite of his earlier gluttony, a large femur spanned his mouth.

"For later," he explained to the animals as he departed mutton mouthed.

In their argot, the grasshoppers openly mocked the dog's avariciousness, "You worry about tomorrow, you miss today. What will you do when you have neither?"

"Tomorrow always comes," the dog said.

The grasshoppers nodded, "This is true, but you will not always come with it."

"Then I've missed nothing."

"You missed today," they countered.

"I think I would like that, if missing today meant having fewer conversations with you."

The insects laughed; the dog was such a good sport with them.

The dog walked away. For the grasshoppers, life provided their necessities, and when it did not, the grasshoppers lived life elsewhere. They refused to grasp the dog's preoccupation with meals. Like time and life, food came, and food went.

Of course, the dog *had* to think about his next snack. Between meals, his wondrous appetite enabled him to devour flocks of ducks or geese when the farmer was not looking. More commonly, the dog ate three heaping bowls of kibbles and endlessly whimpered for more.

An unknown animal spat from the darkened trees, "You don't honor your bets, and you take leftovers home. You're nothing but a cur!"

"Never trust a canine."

"Dirty dog!"

"Mutt."

Several animals hurled variations of these insults at the dog. Yet, no plaintiff did anything to stop him from leaving with the bone or to force him into honoring his debts. The masses were having too good of a time to war. As the dog bid farewell, it became apparent that this event did not mark the dog's first time to renege wagers.

A dismissive grin on his jowls, the dog replied, "Shame on you for trusting me. Again. And again." His jaunt said he was confident that the bamblers still had not learned.

Even the fox took time out from his supervisory duties to wit, "How are you going to take it home?" the party planner asked.

"In my jaws," said the bewildered dog. "How else would I do it?"

As soon as he asked, the pooch knew the punch line.

"I recommend in a doggie bag!"

Gleeful peals erupted throughout the remnants of the party as the pun was retold in guest cliques. The stork laughed far too loudly, and the senatorial tortoise permitted himself to smile at the lame joke.

On his way home, the dog strutted. His belly swayed on the path, rocking him from side to side. Dirt caked his paws wet from spilled beverages and vitreous dew. On a low bridge, the grit plaster fell away, and the clicking of his nails on the splintered planks mesmerized him. Mentally he listed the chores that awaited him at the farm. Although he had a mutton joint in his mouth, eating topped the list, followed by assorted other, more tiresome tasks: marking the wagon, counting the flock, ratting the barn. He felt overworked and underappreciated. Special notes indicated those duties that he could procrastinate on. The dog suddenly emerged from his thoughts. He saw movement off to the side. Past the railing. In the water. He stopped to examine this curiosity.

What luck! A pink and meaty bone rested in the jaws of a scruffy, albeit handsome, dog.

"I think I can take it from him."

The dog paced the bridge. When the dogs' eyes were not locked, they gazed at the others' bone. Both slobbered clear and clotted despite being well-filled, overly satiated.

Longingly longing longer into the running river, the dog decided, "I can definitely get that bone."

He placed his own morsel on the bridge slats to chase the other dog's food.

Yet when the dog returned his sights to his adversary, he exclaimed, "He put his away too!" His opponent had the same astonished reaction. He obviously hoped to pull the same ruse.

"Oh, I see."

The dog sat on the bridge and stared into the water to analyze his problem.

"I could just leave with my bone and leave that dog with his bone, but a single thigh bone will hardly last me two dinners. I must take his, or else I'll likely starve. Still, I saw how that dog looked when I did not have my bone. I think that he is after my food like I am after his, but that puppy does not intimidate me. I can win. I'll have both. I must have both. I deserve both."

A similar line of thought processed behind those inimical, identical watery eyes. The dog calcified himself.

Thus the dog, committed to the act, formulated a plan as to how to nab the other bone. "If that dog keeps his bone in his mouth when I do, then to get that bone, I have to keep my bone in my mouth at the same time. OK. Simultaneously, he'll be after my bone. Hmm. He shouldn't put up too much of a fight. He looks soft."

The dog snarled at the foreign dog, who grimaced in kind. Although the dog winced and worried, he was positive that the other dog had yielded first.

Bone in mouth. He neared his opponent. The wind held its breath, though the river banks' foliage rustled in expectation. With solid steps, the dog's nails clacked slowly on the bridge boards. Lowering his head, the adversary's head rose to jeer at the dog.

"Perhaps he is a more combative than I assumed," the dog thought as he came to within an inch of his foe. "Courage. Courage and patience," he mumbled around the bone.

Pausing for a moment, a shimmer of schooling fish marred the river-dog's countenance. The bridge-dog perceived this as a weakness.

The dog snapped at his reflection! In that second, two suppers were lost.

Rather, three were. Just as the dog chomped at his own bone, a crocodile lunged from the water to snatch the dog off the bridge. In the bubbling spume of the famished crocodile, the femur jammed the gnashing teeth apart and gave the dog scarce chance to flee with an intact hide. He did so as quickly as possible. The abrupt sprint and the brimming gullet were not friendly. At a healthy distance from the river, the dog's stomach evicted the feast from the past two days. He was left voracious anew and without a single meal.

"That pariah stole my bone! Purloined the food right from my mouth!" the dog incensed. "How dare he! The only reason he bested me is because he sicked his pet crocodile on me. Why does he have a pet crocodile?! If I ever see that dog without his reptile pal, I'll...I'll...well, he just better hope I never meet him again! He used a crocodile to steal my bone! Who does that?!"

As he trudged home, the dog practiced his bites on his lengthening shadow. He wrung imaginary bones from pretend dogs, always winning. He was quite ferocious when alone.

The dog's slow demeanor and broad hips had attracted the crocodile from down river. Waiting, stalking, timing. She crawled closer, bypassing corpulent carp and massive mullet for dog. She had been craving canine since waking up. She had dreamed of tasting them.

"Go easy. Do not disturb the water."

Ironically the fish lives that she had spared were what alerted the dog to her approach and prompted him to act recklessly. No living creature had ever wedged her jaws apart, had ever been so brazen or so brave.

For all her efforts and plans, what had she earned? A tiny bone.

She spat it down the river reproachfully.

Three

Her head low to an eddy, a wolf drank the swirling river. Deep, cool drafts soothed her gastric abyss. The hunger abated for a moment.

"But my pups! What'll they have? They'll waste away if I don't eat soon," she said.

Empty desperation swam through her eyes staring into the water. Her unflattering reputation had prevented her from being invited to the race and its feast. Formerly, the farmers had combed the woods to eradicate wolf packs from the timbers. People had burned whole forests over allegations of wolves decimating livestock. Other animals wanted to be as far from that rumored carnage as possible. The wolf could not blame them for her ostracization. With a family of her own, she troubled herself about their wellness and avoided situations that might endanger them. Though now, she was the danger.

Despite her hunger and worries, memories simpered her muzzle. In the good days, the wolves had ravaged sheep flocks. In the last raid, she had lost her mate. Though the specifics of the incident were unclear even to the wolf herself, her compatriot marauders instilled such fear into the farmers and in the forest that the title of outcast persisted. She maintained a lonely existence.

As she was regretting her fallen fate and the fate of her unblemished young, a bone washed onto the bank. A pink and meaty bone from a large animal. Without a thought as to where it came from or to whom it belonged, the wolf gobbled down the morsel whole. It was too large for her. The femur wedged sideways in her throat. The wolf tried to swallow the bone, thinking that if it could reach her gut she would be fine. The bone secured in her throat. The wolf realized what trouble she was in. Hacking and shaking her head, she could not extract the bone. While the technique worked for tearing out ovine roasts, it proved ineffective against their scraps.

Already weak from malnourishment and further taxed through asphyxiation, the wolf's world whirled around her head. She looked at the ground to steady herself, to establish a reference point. Vortices near the shore exacerbated her dizziness. She clamped her eyes shut and took shallow, unrushed breathes. Eight minutes afterward and surefooted once more, she raised her head and opened her eyes. Along the river's opposite bank, a crane waded.

"Pardon me, Mister Crane," she called as best she could.

"Yes?" the crane replied, not certain of the lean canine. He had overheard her prior mutterings. He knew her plight, knew her needs. He wanted to help but not at the cost of his own life.

"I seem to have gotten a bit of food caught in my throat."

"I know. I watched you wolf it down."

"Haha. Good one." The exerting false laughter hurt her throat. "Could I trouble you to help me remove it?"

"How?" asked the crane.

"Use your comely long bill to pull it out."

"Why should I shove my head past your teeth, inside your head, and down your throat to retrieve food that I can't eat? You might as well make a snack of me while I'm so close to your digestives. That way you would have two meals in one."

The wolf did not hesitate. "I'll reward you."

"With what? How much?"

No scruples barricaded her. She would be saved; it was only a matter of how much salvation would cost her. "I'll give you four bushels of the ripest peaches you've ever seen," bartered the wolf.

"They aren't in season."

"Trust me."

The crane doubted the sly mammal. "From where? Which farmer?"

"Your concern is the bone. Mine is the peaches. The longer we blather, the more this bone embeds itself in my throat."

"Make it five bushels then," the crane countered.

"OK," the wolf barked.

The bird had fallen for her wile but did not know it. She would have said five tons if she had needed to. The crane flew to the wolf on the sandy shore. She sat and spread her jaws. Her tail tip swished the bank, smoothing the rippled grains.

The crane's pin feathers graced the wolf cheeks deftly, determinedly. In his mind, he could taste the drupe's nectar, although his job was not yet begun.

"Angle your mouth toward the light."

The wolf obeyed.

"Why didn't you chew?" the crane asked.

The wolf gargled out a response through her open jaws.

"Don't talk with my head down your face. You think that bone's a nuisance. Would you care for my face rapier stabbing your throat?"

The wolf had a reply but kept it to herself.

"Also I think you have TMJ. Your jaw popped when you opened your mouth. Does it hurt to chew?"

The wolf considered shaking her head, but the crane did not seem to want a dialog, rather only a diatribe. He had started on another subject. The wolf's dental habits.

"When was the last time you flossed? I'm sure you probably have a good excuse for not. Do your gums bleed?"

"I can't floss without thumbs. Besides you have a gizzard, not teeth," the wolf thought. "Why's he asking all these questions when he knows full well I can't answer?"

The wolf asked herself these and other ponderings as a means of distracting herself from her quiescent plight. She thought about the crane: his fishy scent, his demeanor, and a thousand more observations that fled as the crane began tugging at the obstruction. The crane's vermilion plumes struggled and slammed into the wolf's throat. She gagged peristaltic spasms.

A jolt! A jerk! From inside the wolf's jaws came the crane with the bone.

"Thank you!" rasped the wolf.

The bone was the length of the crane's beak and the diameter of his head.

"You're welcome. I'm surprised you didn't choke on me while I was in there."

The crane inhaled the riverine air that was so much cleaner than the reek emanating from the wolf's brackish bowels.

The wolf also breathed. She enjoyed the warm air much like she had the cold river water.

When both were properly aerated, the crane touched on the business of payment.

"My reward, the peaches. When can you deliver them by? I'd prefer the bushels staggered over time if possible. If that's impractical, I'll take them all at once. Either way is fine. Whatever is easier for you." His nonchalance belied his discomfort in discussing reimbursement.

"PEACHES! Count that bone as your reward, bird! The bone and your luck that I didn't bite off your head when it was already so near my fangs. The wolf growled at the crane who flew off after snatching the bone from the sandbank. "Why shouldn't I eat you anyway?"

"Why indeed?" thought the crane.

He serenely lighted onto an oak branch and stared at the wolf, at the life he had saved.

The wolf ignored the bird and returned to her rock den hidden among vermiceous roots mining into granite. Hanging mosses draped the entrance. Evening came as the wolf arrived home. She nursed her pups on what milk remained. The whelps were fluffy, but the wolf felt their scrawny muzzles pricking her drained underside.

She had to catch a meal soon; easy prey was fair game. Even scavenging could not be discounted. In her prime, the wolves predated on sizable game, but alone with bellies to fill, starved arrogance could not be humored. It did not provide meat. The wolf could not be finicky. She had to eat tonight.

Once the three little wolves huddled together in sleep, their mother hunted. Ten minutes later the wolf was half a mile from her den. She had picked up the sour, acidic scent of an animal that was deathly sick, if not already departed.

"Tonight, I will dine," the wolf thought.

Having nabbed the fish earlier that day, the crane was responsible for the red herring whose scent the wolf pursued. Now, she was far enough away from the den that the crane could work uninterrupted. He stooped into the wolf's burrow under crags and among roots, having followed the wolf. The crane tripartited the bone.

Meat scraps had been left on the femur. The bird's breaks revealed unctuous, white marrow that dripped onto the hot liar's floor where the fat melted and steamed. The blind whelps sniffed and wriggled like maggots. Using his smell to locate the pups, the crane fed them the bone fragments. The shards lodged in their throats. The puppies wailed, whined, whimpered. The bone had dug too deeply into one pup's larynx. The faintest yip failed to escape. The crane removed that puppy's bone slightly. The crane left when the pup trio supplicated for the wolf in an idioglossia spoken only between mother and offspring. The wolf heard. Her query had taken her a mile from the den, yet she tore back without the food. The wolf rushed through the dewed ferns and burdocks. Her tongue lolled.

Inside the rugged promontory with her pups, she sensed their predicament. Attempting to remove the objects herself would only choke her young all the more. At least they could breathe, as labored as those breathes were. The wolf knew she could not save the litter. Not alone. She wagged, yet the wolf did not calm herself. In her panic, she did not detect the unusual scent in her den.

She looked for help outside. Among fig foliage, the insidious crane feigned sleep. Spotting the bird, the wolf called.

"Crane, quick I need you to take some...something out of my puppies' throats, please!"

"Like mother like pups?"

"Yes!"

"Strange that you need my help again so soon. It must be karma. What will I get this time? More peaches?"

"Whatever you want! Just please help!"

"How many are there?" the crane inquired.

"How many what?! Peaches?"

"Don't be thick. I know you don't have peaches. How many pups are there? How big is your litter? What is the whelp count?"

"Three," she jittered.

"Three, huh? I'll tell you what." He pecked at an itch beneath his right wing for a full forty-six seconds. "I'll help you if you give me one."

"WHAT?!!"

Poppies and Butterflies - Vincent van Gogh

"Give me one of your puppies now, or you'll lose all three. Mathematically, it's in your best interest. Do you need me to go over the arithmetic with you?"

"What will you do with it?"

The crane could not smile. His face was not built that way, but if he were able to, the crane would have smiled. "Two for the price of one. That's a bargain. You're wasting time."

From inside the den, the whelps wept in whispers.

"Alright but you have to choose which one you take."

"Fine. Bring them out. I'll take my reward first, and afterward take care of the other two. Don't try to negotiate."

Not piercing their scruffs lest she agitate the obstructions, the wolf brought her pups into the night air, the moonlight silver on the crane's plumage and gray on the wolves' coats. The bird descended to the ground without concern for the predator. In fact he ignored her as though she were no more a threat than the ground itself. Less even. At least the ground had substance, had resistance. In her current state, the wolf had nothing but despair.

The crane savored this carefree style, more than he would have savored the peaches. He knew he was the best means of saving her litter. The crane selected the pup methodically. He wedged the least bony one in the fork of two cedar boughs.

"For insurance," he said. The pup's milk teeth scratched his beak during the bone removal procedure. "Must be more careful," he thought.

The crane plucked the bone from the young wolf's throat. It cried with the item's removal.

"What is it?"

The wolf saw the white object but could not identify it.

The crane flew back to the ground, the bone in his mouth. "Do you have these littering your cave?" he asked.

Guilt abashed the wolf's tail. "Yes," she admitted.

The crane shook his beak. The wolf paced distraughtly.

"Just hurry," she pleaded.

Making skilled, faultless work of the other two puppies, all three whined in unison. The three bone shards lay piled before the arcane aperture of the wolf's den. Without a farewell, the crane flew off. He grabbed his prize-wolf along his trajectory. He did not stop but while still in midair simply grabbed the pup out of the tree. The cub mewled across the argent treetops and white-black river. The crying stopped. Her two whelps inhaled fully. The mother wolf pawed at the mounded bones to discover the source of this attempted infanticide. The shards fit together so well...

In vengeful epiphany, the wolf bayed.

Meanwhile, her remaining pups lapped femur fat from the hot earth.

Andante (Sonata of the Stars) - Mikalojus Ciurlionis

They saw, advancing towards them, on the same road, a great number of lights, resembling so many moving stars. Sancho stood aghast at the sight of them, nor was Don Quixote unmoved. The one checked his ass and the other his horse, and both stood looking before them with eager attention. They perceived that the lights were advancing towards them, and that as they approached nearer they appeared larger. Sancho trembled like quicksilver at the sight, and Don Quixote's hair bristled upon his head; but, somewhat recovering himself, he exclaimed: "Sancho, this must be a most perilous adventure, wherein it will be necessary for me to exert my whole might and valor."

"Woe is me!" answered Sancho; "should this prove to be an adventure of goblins, as to me it seems to be, where shall I find ribs to endure?"

"Whatsoever phantoms they may be," said Don Quixote, "I will not suffer them to touch a thread of thy garment: for if they sported with thee before, it was because I could not get over the wall; but we are now upon even ground, where I can brandish my sword at pleasure."

"But, if they should enchant and benumb you, as they did then," quoth Sancho, "what matters it whether we are in the open field or not?"

"Notwithstanding that," replied Don Quixote, "I beseech thee, Sancho, to be of good courage; for experience shall give thee sufficient proof of mine."

"I will, if it please God," answered Sancho; and, retiring a little on one side of the road, and again endeavoring to discover what those walking lights might be, they soon after perceived a great many persons clothed in white.

This dreadful spectacle completely annihilated the courage of Sancho, whose teeth began to chatter, as if seized with a quartan ague; and his trembling and chattering increased as more of it appeared in view; for now they discovered about twenty persons in white robes, all on horseback, with lighted torches in their hands; behind them came a litter covered with black, which was followed by six persons in deep mourning; the mules on which they were mounted being covered likewise with black down to their heels; for that they were mules, and not horses, was evident by the slowness of their pace. Those robed in white were muttering to themselves in a low and plaintive tone.

This strange vision, at such an hour, and in a place so uninhabited might well strike terror into Sancho's heart, and even into that of his master; and so it would have done had he been any other than Don Quixote. As for Sancho, his whole stock of courage was now exhausted. But it was otherwise with his master, whose lively imagination instantly suggested to him that this must be truly a chivalrous adventure. He conceived that the litter was a bier, whereon was carried some knight sorely wounded, or slain, whose revenge was reserved for him alone; he, therefore, without delay couched his spear, seated himself firm in his saddle, and with grace and spirit advanced into the middle of the road by which the procession must pass; and, when they were near, he raised his voice and said: "Ho, knights, whoever ye are, halt, and give me an account to whom ye belong; whence ye come, whither ye are going, and what it is ye carry upon that bier; for in all appearance either ye have done some injury to others, or others to you: and it is expedient and necessary that I be informed of it, either to chastise ye for the evil ye have done, or to revenge ye of wrongs sustained."

"We are in haste," answered one in the procession; "the inn is a great way off, and we cannot stay to give so long an account as you require." Then, spurring his mule, he passed forward.

Don Quixote, highly resenting this answer, laid hold of his bridle and said: "Stand, and with more civility give me the account I demand; otherwise I challenge ye all to battle."

The mule was timid, and started so much upon his touching the bridle, that, rising on her hind legs, she threw her rider over the crupper to the ground. A lacquey that came on foot, seeing the man in white fall, began to revile Don Quixote, whose choler being now raised, he couched his spear, and immediately attacking one of the mourners, laid him on the ground grievously wounded; then turning about to the rest, it was worth seeing with what agility he attacked and defeated them; and it seemed as if wings at that instant had sprung on Rozinante—so lightly and swiftly he moved! All the white-robed people, being timorous and unarmed, soon quitted the skirmish and ran over the plain with their lighted torches, looking like so many masqueraders on a carnival or festival night. The mourners were so wrapped up and muffled in their long robes that they could make no exertion; so that Don Quixote, with entire safety, assailed them all, and, sorely against their will, obliged them to quit the field; for they thought him no man, but the devil from hell broke loose upon them to seize the dead body they were conveying in the litter.

All this Sancho beheld with admiration at his master's intrepidity, and said to himself: "This master of mine is certainly as valiant and magnanimous as he pretends to be."

Continued on page 69

Reflecting

by Ian Butterworth

We live, my Grandfather and I, in a large grey house, past which the buses rattle late into the night. There is an armchair, matching the dull red curtains, positioned so the old man can look into the street. Medical equipment waits in the dusty shadows cast by the tall lamp. The light is dim. I wipe a damp flannel over his chest; push aside his tiny penis, avoiding his eyes as I do so. His skin is the colour of mushrooms. I fear bruising him, as if my fingers will mark his flesh. The nurse left a plastic sheet to place under him as he bathes, but I cannot treat him as if he is a child. A sweet biscuit leans, damp in the saucer of his lukewarm tea.

Without the thick lenses of his ridiculous glasses, now folded by his chair, his eyes are yellow and blank. Without his clothes, once impeccably creased, he has faded away. I love him. In my childhood he held me when my father would not. Through my divorce, he refused to judge, though all else knew that the fault was mine. He took me in, when my wife and children left. He taught me to pray, though I was a man. Only weeks before I had watched him before a room of sixth formers, some intense and keen, others bewildered.

'Was it hard?' one asks, uncomprehending. 'How did you survive?'

'Do you hate them?'

He tells it once more, calm as a tale.

As I gently wipe his skin, he mutters, wisps of remembrance.

'Jacob...Jacob.'

His own Grandfather's name...

I squeezed the words from my mouth. The yard, surrounded by fastidious white gravel, blazing rows of coloured flowers; beyond that the wire, barbed and black against the bleached light of the cold, morning sun; and towers filled with men, pointing guns.

'Jacob...please.'

Grandfather; shaved head with cuts, face raw red where his beard had been torn. Blue striped pants, oversized like a clown, waist-knot clutched in his swollen hand, wooden soled shoes, from which his filthy heels dragged in the dust. This proud Rabbi and scholar. Alone in front of the higgledy-piggledy lines of broken boys and men.

'Spit,' said the soldier, a father to a child, almost reverently. 'Spit on it. Save yourself.'

His kippah, woven and neat, lay in the dust, by my Grandfather's feet. How had he hidden it? Who had betrayed?

'Spit on it.'

'Jacob...Grandfather. Please. Spit!' I daren't speak out loud.

The old man remained still, facing the soldier. Holy words emerged from his mouth.

'Grandfather...'

The words became louder. His voice rang out. He swayed in the dust. He bent at the knee.

The berakhah. We could hear. Grandfather was blessing us all.

The soldier raised his arm, the pistol pointing at Grandfather's face.

I wanted to run to him. I wanted it to stop. But my voice was still.

My Grandfather's eyes open, briefly glisten. Then they return, glassy and blank. I lift his arm, heavy and dull. On the underside remains the number, gouged deep, the ink now faint. How he has suffered. How little we know. The end is close. There is nothing I can do.

###

Please Please Please Shut Up

by

Kevin Tosca

Study for Hell, Artist: John Singer Sargent

A playground sat, diabolical, three floors below Jacob's balcony, below his open sliding glass doors, the ones letting in all that early spring light and blue and wind. He hated this playground. He hated it, but winter had come, the 30-round Midwest winter, and he had forgotten his hate.

The devils playing down there were virtuosos, champion yellers yelling nonsense with an impressive and preposterous gusto, reminding Jacob of an interview where Kurt Vonnegut talked about man's desire—his vain need—to proclaim "Killroy [Vonnegut's Everyman] was here."

Jacob then remembered, from a walk he took earlier that day, another noise machine near Medicine Lake, a little boy on a bridge who kept saying (kept whine-repeating as if his message was necessary to unlock the secrets of the universe) "Mom, come here," "Come here, Mom," "Mom," "Mom, look," "Look, Mom," "Mom!" because said mother was on the other side of the bridge tending to the boy's sister, ignoring him.

Is that it? Is that what life is? *All* it is? Are we all just a bunch of large children groping for attention? Desperately needing to be heard? People the world over are (at this and every minute) frenziedly blogging, facebooking, tweeting, texting. They are talking and talking and talking.

A fear shot through Jacob's gut. What if his writing were the same? What if it and all the other arts were merely more sophisticated forms of screaming "Look at me!" "Hear me!" "Somebody, please, recognize my individuality, my worth, my existence—Now!"

Jacob didn't want to be that dependent, that needy, that obvious, that egocentric, that common. He didn't want to be another howling man-child, another pathetic male on the bridge pleading for female attention. And he definitely didn't want to be the artist who needed to say "I lived," either, because he could perceive how incredibly vain and impotent and downright near-sighted that was.

Besides, wasn't he always proud of himself the *less* he spoke at the restaurant where he traded his time for money? Didn't he take a sly, deep pleasure from keeping things hidden there and everywhere? Didn't he feel he betrayed his innermost self, that he lost something vital, when he spoke about what was dearest to him?

So?

So silence. Beautiful, peaceful silence. The sloughing off of all that foolishness and the ability to hear the light and blue and wind and not sully it with your inane ambitions and juvenile needs, your beggary of words. Others would speak, others would *always* speak, so why join the blabbering crowd? Why not just listen and feel and do everyone the favor of not opening your mouth, not filling the air with more oral excrement stamped with your personal brand of want? Why not just shut the fuck up, once and for all?

Jacob smiled, there on his floor. And the children, as they do, went away, but he knew more would come. In this they were like Jehovah's Witnesses, or hard wind. He pulled the comforter off the bed because (despite the calendar's date) the air was cold, and he took a nap, there on his floor.

Later, while eating dinner alone at his kitchen table, Jacob turned on National Public Radio and heard Terry Gross interviewing a historian who had Amyotrophic lateral sclerosis, ALS, otherwise known as Lou Gehrig's disease. The man had suffered more than any being should have to suffer, but he was alive, he could still do a thing or two, and the thing, he said, that he could still do, that mattered most to him, was speak. He said that as bad as it's gotten, it's still okay, but if it gets worse—if it gets to the point where he could no longer talk—*then* he would want to die. The one thing keeping this broken man alive, this man's greatest spiritual pleasure, was talking. Silence to him equaled death, equaled, he intimated, something *worse* than death.

But was this man a child? This learned, honest, vulnerable man who was still writing his books, still teaching his classes, still giving his interviews, still filling the air with his words? There was something defiantly moving and touching about his life: his will, his battles, his simple wish—his need—to communicate. But there was also something undignified, something unwise, something overwhelmingly sad and disgustingly clingy and desperate about him too.

After dinner, Jacob went to see Atom Egoyan's latest film. He watched it alone except for a couple petting and snuggling and making love sounds two rows below him. The film—full of jealousies, insecurities, suspicions and sex—pushed his intellectual and emotional buttons, and he left the theater with a clear, sharpened mind, left it with that and with an intense, urgent desire which made him laugh a wistful, self-scornful laugh.

What did Jacob so intensely, so urgently, want to do? Jacob wanted so intensely and so urgently to share his thoughts, wanted to share them and the whole trajectory of his day, or else what, he demanded, was it worth? What did it—any and all of it—matter?

Jacob went home and he did what a solitary, literary-minded man like him could do on a cold, moon-full, child-vacated early spring midnight night like that: He picked up his pen. When he was through, he re-read what he had written. The words pleased him, and he thanked the silence because he knew the silence was to thank, making Jacob think of another of Vonnegut's themes: the loneliness of man. Utter. Inescapable. Heartbreaking. That, all that, and the paradox. The fact that Jacob wouldn't have written a word, not one lousy letter, if he had talked to someone, shared his day with someone, but he still, yes, he still wanted to share it. Perhaps, God forbid and God damn it to hell, he needed to.

###

An Hour Early

by

Daniel Clausen

I always leave at least an hour or so earlier than the others. They'll go on drinking long after I've left. Drunk, I start to walk home. Soon I'm doing a little jog. Then I'm walking again. I'm not going to be a drunk, like my father, I say, silently in my head until thoughts break out into words. Now I'm talking to myself. I think about doing a Yoda impression for good measure. The ground beneath my feet is moist and sticky, but I have no recollection of it raining. I think the most logical thing in my head just to prove that I can. Then I rant about how great I am—real megalomaniac stuff. I say one day I'll write a novel. As soon as I say it outloud, I'm suddenly depressed. Now, I'm alone on the long path that goes along the Catholic high school to my apartment. The cross at the top of the building isn't menacing or comforting or anything. It's just there. I bust out with a few karate moves. When I'm about to cry, I try to convince myself that I don't love this girl I just met a few weeks ago and that any minute now I can fall into my twenty-third year of life like it's all some big debauch. Drinking, wild sex, and public nudity to top it all off. I stop to write all this down on a little notepad in my pocket, crazy as I am drunk, but not my father in any way, and continue on my way. An hour early, I feel like I'm always getting home late.

Especially for his 'October wind' and 'the loud hills of Wales'.

Editorial by Oonah V Joslin

Stork's Bill by Charles Rennie Mackintosh

ctober 27th 2014 marks the 100th anniversary of one of the greatest wordsmiths of the English language. Dylan Thomas was born in Swansea, South Wales and died in New York 39 years later, leaving us a legacy of words that was worthy of a place in Poet's Corner but he was such a 'bad boy', he didn't get his plaque until 1982. And perhaps it was also because he was a bad boy that I was unaware of his work until 1972 when an enlightened English teacher played us a recording of

"Reminiscences of Childhood" read by Richard Burton – and it seemed he read this just for me;

"The lane was the place to tell your secrets; if you did not have any,
you invented them; I had few. Occasionally, now, I dream that I am
turning, after school, into the lane of confidences where I say to the
children of my class, "At last I have a secret." "What is it ? What is it ?"
"I can fly!" And when they do not believe me, I flap my arms like a
large, stout bird and slowly leave the ground, only a few inches at
first, then gaining air until I fly, like Dracula in a schoolboy cap, level
with the windows of the school, peering in until the mistress at the piano
screams"

"Reminiscences of Childhood"

In that moment I had no idea, that *"ugly, lovely,"* town, *"along the bent and Devon-facing seashore"* would become *alive* to me within a decade; or that I had already fallen in love with Welshness; the richness of tone, hyperbole, bathos and hoyle ~ that deft and empathetic observation of human kind that has in it so much heart.

"And I saw in the turning so clearly a child's
Forgotten mornings when he walked with his mother
Through the parables
Of sun light
And the legends of the green chapels

And the twice told fields of infancy
That his tears burned my cheeks and his heart moved in mine."

"Poem in October"

In the very month of Dylan Thomas' dying, another boy was born in Swansea and he too lived within sound of Cwmdonkin Park, though on the upper side at Townhill, and the within sight of the dockyards. And it really does feel from up on Pantycelyn Rd. that could fly over the town. I married him and I walked often in that park with his grandmother and her Jack Russell Terriers, Bunty and Jane, past the Dylan Thomas memorial garden there; the little brook and stone inscribed with the final words of "Fernhill":

"Oh as I was young and easy in the mercy of his means,
Time held me green and dying

Though I sang in my chains like the sea."

I think I didn't appreciate any of that as I do now. This is the curse of youth and the blessing of age. Later I really began to read his work and in last year's centenary of his death to reread and apply myself properly to his poetry.

Thomas's themes are universal. His language is a gourmet feast of sounds that satisfies the soul. His structuring is so subtle it is not immediately apparent but studying his techniques brings rich rewards. He grabs you and holds you, mesmerised until he has told his story whether in poem or prose, but always with drama:

" the metronome falls with a clout to the ground, stops, and there is no more Time;"

The music of Cymraeg is potent even in dilution.

Wales is a land lavish in contrasts; lofty mountains cover cathedral caves, copper and gold lie with slate and coal. It is dramatic, moody and untamed; a dragon lies twisted round its root. This was the land that nurtured the complex emotions of the man – grandiose yet lacking self esteem, confident in his genius but always exaggerating his own flaws; a sickly child who knew no boundaries; by turns compassionate and careless of all.

In his 1941 sonnet "Among Those Killed in the Dawn Raid was a Man Aged a Hundred", Dylan Thomas celebrated, not the heroic death of a soldier but the life of a civilian. A man of a hundred summers killed in a moment of violence which he highlights thus:

"He put on his clothes and stepped out and he died," (line2)

That is so powerful in its simplicity yet the contrast of *"stepped out and died"* and *"he stopped a sun"* (line 6), stuns and tears at the soul and makes us feel the weight of this one death among the many.

"the spade's ring on the cage" (line11) might be the ring of a mine cage and shovel, or rib cage and gravedigger.

Here was a man who'd loved, lived long, fought his own life's battles and was cut down pitilessly at dawn.

"Tell his street on its back he stopped a sun" says Thomas.
   Great age deserves a celebrated end!

'Time's up,' is a recurring theme in his poetry and he will not have this old man "go gentle." The storks at
   the end of the poem make each year of his life seem a rebirth.

        By contrast, in "Ceremony After the Raid"

"Among the street burned to tireless death
A child of a few hours"

is almost an act of un-creation ~ a life denied identity except as an eternal soul; a life unlived. Study that one
   closely for yourself.

        Dylan Thomas succumbed to his own struggles and wasn't with us long but his words remain and will
illuminate, loudly, hundreds of years to come. All I do here is to honour his struggles and his work with
the final words of "Among Those Killed…"

   "The morning is flying on the wings of his age
   And a hundred storks perch on the sun's right hand"

                            ###

Ash by James Graham

At the grave there is no poetry in me.
The man in the black suit hands me a little box.
Her name is on it. She is ash.

No longer a dead woman with closed eyes
and a cold hand I could still hold.
They place the corpse in the retort.
The burning takes two hours.
All organs and soft tissue vaporise
and are expelled into the air.
The calcined bones are pulverised.
This is the dry narrative that fills my head
instead of poetry. I hold the little box
with her name on it, and put it in the earth.
Later, much later, I begin
ham-fistedly to cram this grief
into a slow-marching metre,
but grief is not in the verse
any more than time is in the clock.
I try to find a metaphor
that is more than a mere trinket:
She was a mile-deep mine.
Seam below seam of priceless ore.
Of kindness: of patient listening
to anxious friends, who went away
assured. Of beauty: fierce dislike
of tawdriness; a gift for making
a sad room, or an old song, lovely.
Of insight: a witty understanding

of the rare wisdom and common folly
of famous men. Of short-lived anger
and spontaneous reconcilement.

These did not age. These skipped
and tumbled like a six-year-old, even as
the mechanisms of the body failed.
I must conjure poems. Poetry
does not work miracles, yet sometimes
makes a good pretence of it
and memory and vision may yet recall
from the chimney-smoke and the dry ash
shards that will merge at last into a ghost
whose voice I can believe I hear.

Ghost by James Graham

It was a quiet time. The passing car, the snap
of the letterbox, gave way to silence. I filled
the bins with papers, plastics, cans. The house

was empty. I served tea and cakes to guests,
Come in, it's good to see you. They filled
the house with talk, and left it silent.

But memory has courage now. Traces begin
to seem not lost but there: her hazel eyes
a little down in disappointment, to the left in thought,
or luminous in nimble understanding, or soft

with gentle love. Her voice, as if
recorded, her *Hel-*lo, her *I don't
think? so,* all her laughs. Her eyes

in my mind's eye, her gentle voice
contending with the silence. This
is a good phantom, passing every day
from room to room, making grief lie still.

LETTER TO MY GRANDMOTHER by Annette Volfing

You slept in curlers. I would run my fingers
over the grooves in your scalp – just as I liked
to rub your toes, moulded by silly shoes.

Now, at the barbers, I ask for a number four.
Maybe that's why, in my dreams,
when you come back like Lazarus,

there's always something wrong – as though it's me
who's gone past recognition, leaving you
unsure of what to say before you fade.

But let me reassure you that the things
you feared for me did not pan out: I haven't been
held back by wanting children, or bad men.

No factory work for me. I've never washed
landings and stairs in blocks on Østerbro.
I know these very words should make

no sense to you, yet like to think
that where you are now, English is possible –
and time to read, and sit.

AGAIN by Annette Volfing

It takes no more
than a certain tilt of the head,
a big nose or a sleek bob,
for me to think,
'Oh, there's Liz on the bus.'

Even though her copies
of Wolfram and Heine
now stand on my shelf,
I still think,
'We'll catch up at lunch.'

ROSES by Annette Volfing

I: Meeting House Garden

Little mouths, yellow with scarlet veins,
so tight and fit.
They hiss like baby snakes
as I go in.

In here, we don't refer to sin. Outside,
the branches whisper; forked tongues speak
to my condition.

II: Windrose

The compass spins, the sky is all
white light. Who cares which way
we blow?

Leviathan is far below.

III: The Recipe

The rose – over time it has been named,
romanced and plucked. And now cut up,
the petals ground to make pink salt.

This rose, at least, will not get sick.
The crystals keep the worm at bay.

Black Overcoat by Ian C Smith

When I fail to produce a return ticket to the past
my people look askant or slyly at each other.
I know my archness, puns, jokester's life views,
cause their wariness of being duped.
I forget to think of kindness, their wellbeing.
Can't remember sounds like a guilty plea.
The black overcoat of amnesia does nothing
to ward off isolation's chill, however deserved.

I lurch up from lunatic dreams looking slantwise
to find objects in damned absurd places.
If I weren't diligently writing things down
yesterday would turn to ash, no nearer
than the sad, enchanted days of a boy,
his precious tattered books, the whispering girls
sneaked past his stone-faced landlady,
the long shadows down her hallway.

Even before the drama of hospital diagnosis
reading what I had written seemed more real
than the details of what took place.
A Sussex churchyard, at Thomas Gray's grave,
his elegy about ordinary lives famous,
my ripple of remembrance is without context.
Writing it fixed that pilgrimage in my mind.
My ravaged memory is now ordinary.

Enough of the past surfaces to remind me
that though my days must wind to an end
I have felt the rain on my face we each crave.
Above a green valley I hear the wind's song
rushing past on my glider joy flight,
a memory like a scene in a film.
I shrug reverie, hunt down fugitive glasses,
write about my mind's windmills.

Literary Vagabond by Ian C Smith

Each story offends in a different way,
scaring the bejeezus out of publishers.
His scandalous stripping of sacred taboos,
the raw exposés, scald even the printers.
He banjaxes Ireland, insults the English king,
suffers fits, ulcers, and eye problems,
and complains to the newspapers.

His plan to canvass Dublin's publicans,
a literary pub-crawl with a publisher
to sweet talk them so they won't sue,
stirs pettifoggery, and, in turn, his paranoia.
Envious fellows, back-stabbers like him,
spread stories of Nora's liberties,
crazing him cruelly with sexual jealousy.

Using a suitcase lid on his knees as a desk
he composes his gallimaufry of those streets
into *Ulysses*, in their Swiss bedroom.
By night he carouses with cronies,
vexing Nora, bored by artists, neglect, and exile.
When Sylvia Beach finally publishes the epic
Nora, who never finishes it, sells her signed copy.

Rue has a bitter scent by Ian C Smith

Picture a Metro station's harsh stage lights.
She turns and walks away without a fight
or looking back at me, statue-still.
I feel my heart rush, our taut happiness
vanishing down the gusty tunnel's throat.

I don't throw away a cigarette that afternoon,
nor wear a trenchcoat with a snap-brim hat,
this isn't an entertainment by Graham Greene,
just me acting egotistically,
my outburst not quite a public scene.

Throughout the ramifying silence since,
the calmness of books jostled by rowdy flashbacks
known only to me in my melancholic urge
to chase the shadows of tangled moments;
I yearn to re-enact that foolish strife.

In the pre-dawn hours we need a helpline to talk us
back up the long slide of years to the silly songs,
to those rumbling stations of the past where
we put things right, correct our bitter wrongs,
see faces we never saw again and don't deserve to see.

Apprehension by Stan Long

   Consider
the inner eye that part of us
still attached
to the genesis of being
   first
an apprehension a not quite
seeing a not quite believing
   more
an expectation awaiting
confirmation
   until
the mind
made consciousness
its reality
the corporeal eye
the eye of the cosmos
   this
ability
a nascent quality of matter
how else explain
the origin of life the Big Bang
   all
things sprung from it
galaxies planets out of the
   nothing-
ness life evolved
an eye appeared looked on
to see what happened

Certain Stimuli by Jeff Jeppessen

road construction and the smell of hot tar
is those days in fourth or maybe
fifth grade when we had extended recesses
because fumes from the tar used by the roofing guys permeated the school
drove all of us outdoors
students and teachers and librarians

me and some other boys hunkered in these big round concrete
tunnel pieces on the playground
scrawled with older kids' graffiti
shady and cool on those hot afternoons

so we hung out in the rings and complained about the awful smell
how it burned the nose and throat
we talked also of important things
laughed and snorted like well
kids although we knew we weren't

I'm sure it was mainly about girls and cigarettes
what the bad words and drawings
splashed on the insides of the concrete rings
might really mean
do you think it really looks like that?

we swore up and down
we would never ever do
the same cruel things our parents did
right now the burning at the back of the throat
stinging eyes
is just fumes from hot tar

WHEN THE MORNING IS A PRAYER by Kathleen Cassen Mickelson

How do I talk about fresh snow
that still delights me after a lifetime
of Minnesota winters or the sliver
of moon embedded in pre-dawn
sky or the way oak limbs hold
frost to cover their leafless-ness?

It all fills me as if I am unwrapping
gift after gift after gift.
Sunrise viewed from our bedroom
window while our old red dog
leans against my right side, my hand
on her head, light beneath crows'
wings as they cross my vision. I can hear
them, hear the dog breathe, house
sigh, and you creak the mattress

as you turn over to ask me
what I see.

LEARNING TO MAKE PICKLES by Kathleen Cassen Mickelson

August in the kitchen, humid
inside and out. Blue jays have squawked
all summer, their azure and gray bodies
appearing on the deck chairs, on the lips
of plant containers, their discordant songs
a rasp through hazy air.

My search for stock pots
large enough to hold
canning jars on racks
has consumed the past two days.
Cucumbers, picked this morning, lie
sliced in my biggest bowl, mixed
with onions, pickling salt, and three
cloves of garlic.

Last night, I listened to a local poet
talk about beauty in daily details.
She should come to my kitchen, sit
at the counter while I muddle
through my first canning experience.

I hope I don't make a mistake.

Just last weekend I learned my mother canned food
before I was born, saved something of summer.
Was this really the same woman who
sometimes burned Totino's Frozen Pizza
on Saturday nights because she did not
want to stand in the kitchen
to keep watch?

Show me the connection.

I know I am her daughter in ways
I dislike yet I've come to appreciate
her more of late, realized there is so much
I do not know about my introverted
secretly feminist mother. Sometimes
a discordant blue jay song triggers an
image of her dissatisfied face as she stared
at the parenting role before her, as she wished
for nothing but to be
left alone.

Sometimes I see her staring back at me
from my own daughter's face
and it scares me.

Cooking is my armor, my dam that stops the flow
of memory that holds early definitions
of myself. I seal today's efforts,
freshly sliced, in sterile glass jars, place
them on a shelf.

Come winter, the blue jays will still
be here, stark against the snow, silenced to me
by closed windows. Then, I will open
a simple jar of pickles, savor this
small attempt at preserving
all that is good.

The Basket Weaver by Clare McCotter
for Eimear Bradley

There are no wild geese circling this basket
no mountain ranges or quail plumes
only hues of pussy willow and hazel
woven into a child's sun.
Buff and green and silvery blue
turned slowly like the old worshippings
now sidewalls rise to rim lined with seed beads.

Keen as the scent of horses in first frost
she came to the big house newly qualified.
Other occupational therapists
cracking up when she asked
who wants to make a basket?
Didn't she know that stuff was old hat?
It was all about assessment
Beck Depression Scales and risk management.
Hands working wicker a thing of the past.

Being a bona fide basket case
with a differential diagnosis of totally spaced
I accepted her offer.
Sculpting sticks and air into a gourd used
to hold thoughts crackling in gold and scarlet.
Poured out across the fields at dusk
with a spoke of sallow prayer:

O let the starless night begin
And beginning quiet all the voices.

Thoughts of a tortoise before killing a playwright by Barry Charman

In this dream
I am reincarnated
As the tortoise
Falling from the eagle's grasp
Who collides with Aeschylus
And knocks him dead

I do not want him dead
I simply have no control
As I fall
I worry about the anecdotal quality
Of the following moments
And the poor man's
Shock

I have enough time to wonder
Why *this* dream
What thoughts are trying to surface
From what stress?
What is there going unsaid?

Or perhaps I am a tortoise
All along
Over-thinking
My part
And giving way to unhelpful
Meditations as I fall

Elderflower Moon by Sheree Mack

Under the elderflower moon,
you should look for me within
the swollen loch.

Beside the waving flags of reeds,
you will see me swimming from
the fabric of the shore.

In the shadow of trees,
you should listen for distant
laughter rippling across the mirror.

Porcelain Prisoner by Marilyn Hammick

Grandpa hands me his stick, stretches
for the cup *- the last one, lift it child -*
as if I don't know what to do, as if
this is the first time the woman
who lives at its waist has lifted

her skirts in my face,
has begged to be freed
from the kitchen dresser
in Monkey Tree House
where she keeps company

with odd buttons, collar studs,
a shilling for the meter, recalling
how rumba shakers in Panama City
cut at the isthmus of her dreams.

- the last one, lift it child - of course, I reply
and the lady and I follow the cup, stick and coffin.

Smerwick by Bernadette McCarthy

'...the Scandinavians used 'butter' as a term of praise for land...It appears that Muirbech was originally the name for the whole bay and its coastline, and that *smjör-vik* is an Old-Norse realisation.'
Sheehan, J., Stumann Hansen, S., and Ó Corráin, D. 2001. 'A Viking Age maritime haven: a reassessment of the island settlement at Beginish, Co. Kerry'.

You stop on the moon-slick sand
and turn to Ballinrannig.
'There's too much light'.
A stone's throw between us
then another, and another
as you skim back the strand
to check the electric blanket.

I stare at the amber smear
of windowpanes and wonder
did those women feel the same
stone-slump in the belly
as the butter *vik* was consumed
by a Northern fleet?

A wheyed shade, slipshodding,
curds up into you.

Lamb's Ear by Bernadette McCarthy

We were Mrs Coughlan's communion class.
Tom was slow. One morning he bore
a lamb's ear in its first flourish
that was passed between caffling hands,
in wonder that God should furnish
baby ears for brazen ditches,
to be rasped crude by cows' tongues.

I rubbed the lobe. Tender as a bruise:
a fondling, reluctant to be schooled.

harsh sunlight
on the fourth anniversary
of his death
sunrise on the lough
almost painful to watch

Any Given Day   by Judy Brackett

On any given day
    (not that they're not all given,
    they're certainly not earned or won,
    but sometimes stumbled upon while
    we slog through the last of yesterday
    or make lists for tomorrow
    and the days after)
there'll be 3 or 5 or 7
    (almost always an uneven number, but
    why "uneven" as if those are lesser
    things or days or troublesome or awkward
    things or days, though possibly more interesting
    compared to the "evens," those 2s and
    8s and 24s, which might connote
    boring, drugged, half-asleepish,
    square and settled
    and safe)
big-eared, big-eyed, black-tail-twitching,
tick-ridden deer, ambling through this wildish acre
to or from the creek
    (no odds or evens in their lives, though
    isn't it presumptuous to say what's
    even or odd for them)
browsing everything fresh and green—
including the deer-proof, deer-resistant
    (just the sight of them, 3 or 5 or 7,
    the watcher's joy/despair as they spring
    over the fence and sample the Bibb,
    the Swiss chard...never
    the kale or arugula, never
    the daffodils)
ignoring the NotTonightDeer spray,
ignoring the pantyhose filled
with the barber's urine-sprinkled clippings
(not necessarily the barber's own urine),
staring down the dog, even seeming to pose
for the ridiculous camera, their dark, impassive eyes
filled with beauty and deep old danger, and finally
turning and bounding off, leaving the watcher
with rueful thanks for this day's rewards—
chomped-off veggies, trampled pansies,
ticks, sunny daffodils, and bitter kale.

at low tide
the sound of seagulls
and moaning wind
in the rock pool I find nothing
but my reflection
msclarke

The Colors of Desire by Judy Brackett

A craving is wet isn't it
briny chartreuse
except when it's
cobalt wearing
a moonsheen

It's an inhalation
a clenching
a sort of fist

It's those few seconds
before you wake
when then and soon and now
possess you
your desires
mundane and strange
and you want all of it
yesterday
tomorrow
and this oval
cobalt moment

From page 36...

A burning torch lay upon the ground near the first whom the mule had overthrown, by the light of which Don Quixote espied him, and going up to him, placed the point of his spear to his throat, commanding him to surrender, on pain of death.

To which the fallen man answered: "I am surrendered enough already, since I cannot stir, for one of my legs is broken. I beseech you, sir, if you are a Christian gentleman, do not kill me: you would commit a great sacrilege, for I am a licentiate and have taken the lesser orders."

"Who the devil, then," said Don Quixote, "brought you hither, being an ecclesiastic?"

"Who, sir?" replied the fallen man; "my evil fortune."

"A worse fate now threatens you," said Don Quixote, "unless you reply satisfactorily to all my first questions."

"Your worship shall soon be satisfied," answered the licentiate; "and therefore you must know, sir, that though I told you before I was a licentiate, I am in fact only a bachelor of arts, and my name is Alonzo Lopez. I am a native of Alcovendas, and came from the city of Baeza with eleven more ecclesiastics, the same who fled with the torches. We were attending the corpse in that litter to the city of Segovia. It is that of a gentleman who died in Baeza, where he was deposited till now, that, as I said before, we are carrying his bones to their place of burial in Segovia, where he was born."

"And who killed him?" demanded Don Quixote.

"God," replied the bachelor, "by means of a pestilential fever."

"Then," said Don Quixote, "our Lord hath saved me the labor of revenging his death, in case he had been slain by any other hand. But, since he fell by the hand of Heaven, there is nothing expected from us but patience and a silent shrug; for just the same must I have done had it been His pleasure to pronounce the fatal sentence upon me. It is proper that your reverence should know that I am a knight of La Mancha, Don Quixote by name, and that it is my office and profession. to go over the world righting wrongs and redressing grievances."

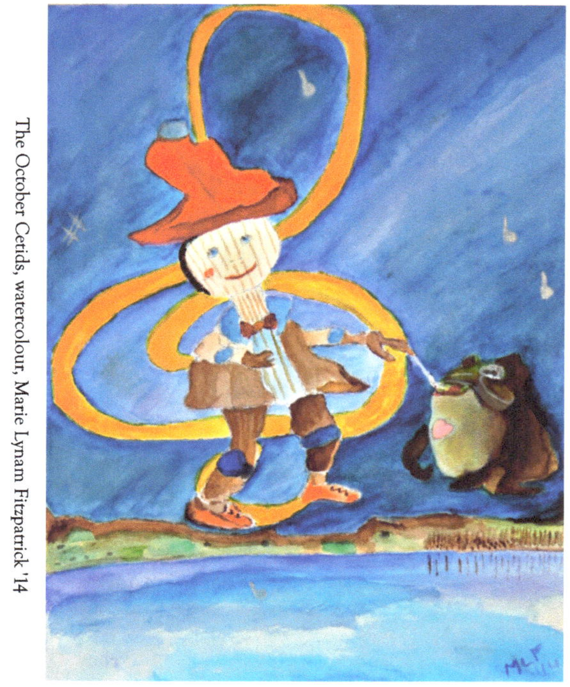

The October Cetids, watercolour, Marie Lynam Fitzpatrick '14

Every Stick

by

Bill West

A scarecrow in a stovepipe hat fiddled and danced a jig. Discordant notes sharp as star frost. He thumped the earth with twiggy feet and croaked his garbled song. The wind whipped the dirge away through empty skies. No owls blinked time from the skeletal trees, no gulls mewed the chorus whilst skimming barren waves. His bow was smooth, his fiddle unstrung. He whirled and spun~counted time with his jerking limbs.

A toad, fat as a truck, popped its eyes. Mesmerised. Its tongue flicked, and licked him up.

Every stick.

...

The Deadly Poppy Field

Excerpt: The Wonderful Wizard of Oz
by L. Frank Baum

Chapter 8

Poppy Field in a Hollow near Giverny by Claude Monet

Our little party of travelers awakened the next morning refreshed and full of hope, and Dorothy breakfasted like a princess off peaches and plums from the trees beside the river. Behind them was the dark forest they had passed safely through, although they had suffered many discouragements; but before them was a lovely, sunny country that seemed to beckon them on to the Emerald City.

To be sure, the broad river now cut them off from this beautiful land. But the raft was nearly done, and after the Tin Woodman had cut a few more logs and fastened them together with wooden pins, they were ready to start. Dorothy sat down in the middle of the raft and held Toto in her arms. When the Cowardly Lion stepped upon the raft it tipped badly, for he was big and heavy; but the Scarecrow and the Tin Woodman stood upon the other end to steady it, and they had long poles in their hands to push the raft through the water.

They got along quite well at first, but when they reached the middle of the river the swift current swept the raft downstream, farther and farther away from the road of yellow brick. And the water grew so deep that the long poles would not touch the bottom.

"This is bad," said the Tin Woodman, "for if we cannot get to the land we shall be carried into the country of the Wicked Witch of the West, and she will enchant us and make us her slaves."

"And then I should get no brains," said the Scarecrow.

"And I should get no courage," said the Cowardly Lion.

"And I should get no heart," said the Tin Woodman.

"And I should never get back to Kansas," said Dorothy.

"We must certainly get to the Emerald City if we can," the Scarecrow continued, and he pushed so hard on his long pole that it stuck fast in the mud at the bottom of the river. Then, before he could pull it out again--or let go--the raft was swept away, and the poor Scarecrow left clinging to the pole in the middle of the river.

'Good-bye!" he called after them, and they were very sorry to leave him. Indeed, the Tin Woodman began to cry, but fortunately remembered that he might rust, and so dried his tears on Dorothy's apron.

Of course this was a bad thing for the Scarecrow.

"I am now worse off than when I first met Dorothy," he thought. "Then, I was stuck on a pole in a cornfield, where I could make-believe scare the crows, at any rate. But surely there is no use for a Scarecrow stuck on a pole in the middle of a river. I am afraid I shall never have any brains, after all!"

Down the stream the raft floated, and the poor Scarecrow was left far behind. Then the Lion said:

Something must be done to save us. I think I can swim to the shore and pull the raft after me, if you will only hold fast to the tip of my tail."

So he sprang into the water, and the Tin Woodman caught fast hold of his tail. Then the Lion began to swim with all his might toward the shore. It was hard work, although he was so big; but by and by they were drawn out of the current, and then Dorothy took the Tin Woodman's long pole and helped push the raft to the land.

They were all tired out when they reached the shore at last and stepped off upon the pretty green grass, and they also knew that the stream had carried them a long way past the road of yellow brick that led to the Emerald City.

"What shall we do now?" asked the Tin Woodman, as the Lion lay down on the grass to let the sun dry him.

"We must get back to the road, in some way," said Dorothy.

"The best plan will be to walk along the riverbank until we come to the road again," remarked the Lion.

So, when they were rested, Dorothy picked up her basket and they started along the grassy bank, to the road from which the river had carried them. It was a lovely country, with plenty of flowers and fruit trees and sunshine to cheer them, and had they not felt so sorry for the poor Scarecrow, they could have been very happy.

They walked along as fast as they could, Dorothy only stopping once to pick a beautiful flower; and after a time the Tin Woodman cried out: "Look!"

Then they all looked at the river and saw the Scarecrow perched upon his pole in the middle of the water, looking very lonely and sad.

"What can we do to save him?" asked Dorothy.

The Lion and the Woodman both shook their heads, for they did not know. So they sat down upon the bank and gazed wistfully at the Scarecrow until a Stork flew by, who, upon seeing them, stopped to rest at the water's edge.

"Who are you and where are you going?" asked the Stork.

"I am Dorothy," answered the girl, "and these are my friends, the Tin Woodman and the Cowardly Lion; and we are going to the Emerald City."

"This isn't the road," said the Stork, as she twisted her long neck and looked sharply at the queer party.

"I know it," returned Dorothy, "but we have lost the Scarecrow, and are wondering how we shall get him again."

"Where is he?" asked the Stork.

"Over there in the river," answered the little girl.

"If he wasn't so big and heavy I would get him for you," remarked the Stork.

"He isn't heavy a bit," said Dorothy eagerly, "for he is stuffed with straw; and if you will bring him back to us, we shall thank you ever and ever so much."

"Well, I'll try," said the Stork, "but if I find he is too heavy to carry I shall have to drop him in the river again."

So the big bird flew into the air and over the water till she came to where the Scarecrow was perched upon his pole. Then the Stork with her great claws grabbed the Scarecrow by the arm and carried him up into the air and back to the bank, where Dorothy and the Lion and the Tin Woodman and Toto were sitting.

When the Scarecrow found himself among his friends again, he was so happy that he hugged them all, even the Lion and Toto; and as they walked along he sang "Tol-de-ri-de-oh!" at every step, he felt so gay.

"I was afraid I should have to stay in the river forever," he said, "but the kind Stork saved me, and if I ever get any brains I shall find the Stork again and do her some kindness in return."

"That's all right," said the Stork, who was flying along beside them. "I always like to help anyone in trouble. But I must go now, for my babies are waiting in the nest for me. I hope you will find the Emerald City and that Oz will help you."

"Thank you," replied Dorothy, and then the kind Stork flew into the air and was soon out of sight.

They walked along listening to the singing of the brightly colored birds and looking at the lovely flowers which now became so thick that the ground was carpeted with them. There were big yellow and white and blue and purple blossoms, besides great clusters of scarlet poppies, which were so brilliant in color they almost dazzled Dorothy's eyes.

"Aren't they beautiful?" the girl asked, as she breathed in the spicy scent of the bright flowers.

"I suppose so," answered the Scarecrow. "When I have brains, I shall probably like them better."

"If I only had a heart, I should love them," added the Tin Woodman.

"I always did like flowers," said the Lion. "They of seem so helpless and frail. But there are none in the forest so bright as these."

They now came upon more and more of the big scarlet poppies, and fewer and fewer of the other flowers; and soon they found themselves in the midst of a great meadow of poppies. Now it is well known that when there are many of these flowers together their odor is so powerful that anyone who breathes it falls asleep, and if the sleeper is not carried away from the scent of the flowers, he sleeps on and on forever. But Dorothy did not know this, nor could she get away from the bright red flowers that were everywhere about; so presently her eyes grew heavy and she felt she must sit down to rest and to sleep.

But the Tin Woodman would not let her do this.

"We must hurry and get back to the road of yellow brick before dark," he said; and the Scarecrow agreed with him. So they kept walking until Dorothy could stand no longer. Her eyes closed in spite of herself and she forgot where she was and fell among the poppies, fast asleep.

"What shall we do?" asked the Tin Woodman.

"If we leave her here she will die," said the Lion. "The smell of the flowers is killing us all. I myself can scarcely keep my eyes open, and the dog is asleep already."

It was true; Toto had fallen down beside his little mistress. But the Scarecrow and the Tin Woodman, not being made of flesh, were not troubled by the scent of the flowers.

"Run fast," said the Scarecrow to the Lion, "and get out of this deadly flower bed as soon as you can. We will bring the little girl with us, but if you should fall asleep you are too big to be carried."

So the Lion aroused himself and bounded forward as fast as he could go. In a moment he was out of sight.

"Let us make a chair with our hands and carry her," said the Scarecrow. So they picked up Toto and put the dog in Dorothy's lap, and then they made a chair with their hands for the seat and their arms for the arms and carried the sleeping girl between them through the flowers.

On and on they walked, and it seemed that the great carpet of deadly flowers that surrounded them would never end. They followed the bend of the river, and at last came upon their friend the Lion, lying fast asleep among the poppies. The flowers had been too strong for the huge beast and he had given up at last, and fallen only a short distance from the end of the poppy bed, where the sweet grass spread in beautiful green fields before them.

"We can do nothing for him," said the Tin Woodman, sadly; "for he is much too heavy to lift. We must leave him here to sleep on forever, and perhaps he will dream that he has found courage at last."

"I'm sorry," said the Scarecrow. "The Lion was a very good comrade for one so cowardly. But let us go on."

They carried the sleeping girl to a pretty spot beside the river, far enough from the poppy field to prevent her breathing any more of the poison of the flowers, and here they laid her gently on the soft grass and waited for the fresh breeze to waken her.

***

SIXTEEN

by

Billy O'Callaghan

Red and Gold Salute Sunset by James Abbott McNeill Whistler

They leave the hotel ballroom soon after midnight, last out into the night except for the band. Two couples in their best clothes, elderly, exhausted but content, drunk with laughter; the men, James and Charlie, wearing tuxedos that have traipsed a few too many good turns but which remain, more by luck than judgement, still the fair side of presentable; and the women, April and Isabelle, in dresses fresh off a peg, sapphire silk to below the knee, ruby suede and long-sleeved satin.

Streetlights burn a shade that fits the late silent hour like a snug vest, a calm nostalgic phosphorescence nearly yellow, nearly white, hiding just enough for time to lose its usual strict delineations.

"That was some night," April says, and venting a deep, happy sigh, slips her arm inside of Isabelle's. Their heels clacking slow flamenco beats against the asphalt, the women skip ahead of the men, though April turns and tosses a smile back over one bare shoulder, to keep them involved or at least biting. "I haven't danced such a night in years. Decades."

"Centuries," Isabelle adds, and laughs.

Charlie raises his right hand and with thumb and fingertips begins to knead his left collarbone. "I'll probably sleep for a week and a half after this. And I'll bet golden eggs that I wake up sore."

"There's a cure for that," says April. "Stay up. Sleep is for the young. At your age, why take a chance?"

"At my age? In case it's slipped your lovely senile little mind, my darling, I'm just two months older than you. Once you've turned passed eighty, two months is a handful of sand snatched from a mile of beach."

"Actually, you're two months and nine days older. If you want to get technical about it."

"I could eat a hamburger," James says, to no one in particular.

"No, you couldn't," Isabelle says.

"With hot mustard, fried onions and extra pickle."

"No, you definitely couldn't."

"And a finger-thick slice of cheddar melted just enough so that the corners turn to rubber."

"Like the nine days make such a difference."

"Nine days can be practically eternal if you spend them wisely. If God had taken nine days to make the world instead of cutting corners in typically slack-assed fashion, just think what He might have achieved."

"Maybe, if He could have kept the unions from getting involved."

"These are still my own teeth, don't forget," James says, snapping his jaw shut a few times in demonstration, compensating by jutting his chin a tad in order to correct the slight overbite. "And I'm still better at eating than dancing."

"Conceded." Isabelle twists her mouth in a way that should make a mess of her beauty. "But that pickle could spell trouble. And I won't even go there with the cheese."

The four friends cross the empty street and start off down the promenade toward the train station. They walk without hurry, knowing that even if they miss one train there'll be another to catch, and free of such troubles they allow their thoughts the freedom of better directions. They have a lit night, companionship, hearts still alive from a recent chasing, and a nearly overwhelming need for talk, teasing, and laughter.

On the station platform, the men find a bench and sit. The women prefer to stand, the elevated advantage affording them something they can't quite define. They are careful, though, to keep out of the direct light. Shadows help to blur the lines.

"It's warm tonight."

James looks up at Isabelle. "July. Midsummer. Of course it's warm."

She shrugs. "Even for July. Even for midsummer. Remember when we were sixteen?"

"Who doesn't remember?" says Charlie. "We close our eyes for five minutes, that's where we want to be. All we do anymore is remember."

"Young and full of the world." April laughs and starts to hum an old tune. After a few bars, Charlie joins in and then begins to sing. The words and melody, unturned by him in three quarters of a lifetime, feel fresh as a longed-for breeze. *Someday, you'll want me to want you...*

"I meant, sixteen on a night like this."

James meets her gaze, and smiles. "Ah. You mean swimming."

She nods. "Swimming."

Charlie breaks the song and they all exchange slow glances. "Well," he says, eventually. "Why the hell not?"

"You know why not." Isabelle straightens the skirt of her dress down over her thighs and knees, then folds her arms across her narrow chest. "We all know."

"I don't."

"Well, you were always a good brick shy of a shed."

"True enough. But in this country, dumbness never disqualified a man from exercising his constitutional rights. So I say, let's put it to a vote." He looks around. "How about it? Who's with me and who's chick-chick-chickadee? A show of hands, please, ladies and cads."

James takes his keys from his jacket pocket, unfolds a thin file from a nail clippers and sets to poking at the cuticle of his right index finger. April drifts away to the brink of the platform and peers back along the line, willing a train to appear and straining to penetrate the gloom of distance.

Charlie slaps his knees. "What's the matter with us?"

"Nothing. Except that it's late and we're old. And it's probably still against the law."

"Swimming is against the law?"

"It is when you're wrapped in nothing but skin."

"We didn't let that stop us when we were sixteen."

"That was our reason for doing it then. Because we were sixteen and looked it."

"I did it to cool down," says Isabelle, her tone playfully haughty.

"Liar." April turns back from the track. "You did it because you wanted to see if these two were even half the men they thought themselves to be."

"And were we?" James asks, smirking.

"Of course not. What boy ever is?"

Isabelle turns on her. "Well, what about you, Little Miss A-plus? Why did you do it?"

"Because I was sixteen, and in love with everything and everyone. And because I was just then coming to life."

"And now?" says Charlie.

"Now," she thinks about it, and shrugs. "Now I've rusted shut." A certain sadness descends, the way fog can suddenly roll in ahead of a hot day, and for an instant, Charlie regrets pushing. Yet he can't bring himself to stop. He needs what this night is holding.

"Come on, sweetheart. There's life in the old cat yet. I saw you tonight. A smile the span of the Golden Gate Bridge and Jazz hands to beat the band."

A giggle floats through Isabelle.

They all turn and stare.

"Spill it," says Charlie, unable to resist his own grin.

She bows her head, but the joy of the thought is evident.

"I was just remembering what happened when you saw me coming out of the water. I'll bet that wouldn't happen now."

"Save it. You'd lose your money in seven seconds flat. Guaranteed. I'm old, not dead."

"Your tongue was nearly to your knees. April thought you were wearing a necktie."

"What can I say? I was smitten. Must have been all that starlight. The poet in me, I suppose."

"The horndog, you mean."

"Well, that's a kind of poetry, too, isn't it? At least, it used to be."

A train rocks into view, its noise repressed to mere vibrations. Empty, half-lit carriages fill the station, doors shudder pneumatically open and gape in wait. Above each, a placename fills the destination window: Greenway. The name awakens memories, of school, friends, family, childhood. Late autumn Carnivals, spring picnics, and those long burning nights of summer, insinuations of transistor radio, porch swings, the smell of cut grass and, huddled in some dark place down by the creek, joyous utterings and the sugary taste of a lover's skin. They sit and stand, waiting for a different train, but their minds are already back there, or already on their way.

"When you're sixteen," James says, softly, "you think you'll live forever. But you don't really believe it. And it's not something you even want. Because who would? Having to go on day after day while the good stuff turns to dust all around you. So when it happens, you don't know how to cope. You try as best you can to be happy, but there's no way of sustaining that, not when you've been to your third funeral of the month and it's still only the fifteenth, or when your hips ache a week in advance of the first November sleet, or when you lie in the dark counting heartbeats and wondering if the next knock will be the last."

April draws back from the edge of the tracks.

"Or when," she says, "after spending five terrible minutes peering at that brittle reflection in a mirror, you dig out the photographs that prove what a beauty you once were, the pictures from school that catch you smiling just right, slightly embarrassed over something someone just whispered but curious, too, and hungry, still able to get excited at the prospect of a ride in a new car or a slow dance with the boy you want to marry."

"Forever is too long," James says, and sighs. "I say let's just do it, damn it. Let's go swimming."

No one speaks on the ride out. Thirty-five elastic minutes. Suburbs pass, then towns, lampposts glow-worming the darkness. And the dreams linger, the time committed in so much detail to memory. Isabelle is right about the heat. James pulls open his bowtie and lets it hang loosely in place, then as the women watch undoes the throat and second buttons of his shirt. A tuft of hair bristles into view, the colour so white that it seems to dull the pure clean boast of his shirt.

They remain seated when the train finally slows. Their station is an open one, a platform, a couple of benches and a long narrow single story clapboard building with two bathrooms, some vending machines and a ticket kiosk. When everything is still again, they rise, step out into the night, and walk westward, to where the ocean waits. The beach is empty, the dark water curling in and away against sand the colour of exposed bone.

"How do we do this?" April asks, laughter quivering her breath.

"The way we did before," says Charlie. He slips off his coat. "Except," he adds, "with one difference. We're old as mummified pharaohs and trying, at least for a little while, to feel like kids again. This is an illusion, with all the delicacy of cobweb. We should agree not to look at one another."

April kicks off her shoes. "Agreed."

Isabelle hesitates, then starts to work open the buttons at the hip of her dress. "Me, too," she sighs. "If that's what it'll take."

They all turn then to James, who has dropped down onto the sand and begun to untie the laces of his shoes. He looks up. "Oh," he says. "Fine with me. I can't see anything anyway. Not without my glasses."

Tonight, the dark is a kindness. They peel off their clothes to the soft lapping of the surf and the occasional distant rumble of a train coming or pulling out. Each stands apart from the rest, gazing only downward or out over the ocean. The sky above is empty, the stars for now hidden. When they are naked, James again starts to sing, his voice held small, his breath driving the melody. "I know that someday you'll want me to want you..."

"Are we ready?" he asks, the words a part of the music, and an arm's length or more apart, they march forward as one, down the strand, into the breaking tide.

The water feels cold, as cold as it ever did and ever will. Charlie begins to laugh.

"Cut it out!" Isabelle squeals, feigning anger. "You can't break your own rules!"

Archie Reaches Too High
(and makes enemies)

by

Bill Frank Robinson

Image: Getting Ready for the Game ~ Artist: Carl Larsson

The clanging bell hammers relentlessly as children pour from the old school house into the bright sun. They hit the street and scatter in all directions, headed home for the day. One little towhead darts through the crowd, running hard. It's Archie Cleebo dressed in bib overalls, man's work shirt, and worn-out tennis shoes. He slows as he approaches a vacant lot. A group of junior high school guys are in the middle of the lot; they're playing marbles. They call themselves the best marble players in town. Archie snorts, they never get beat 'cause they won't play with anybody that might beat 'em. Archie picks up speed and passes the lot. Then, for no reason he knows about, he stops running and walks back to watch the game.

Billy and Arnold Weaver, twin brothers and big fat mean guys, are doing all the talking. Arnold is saying, "Clean the pot, Billy. Show these monkeys what a Weaver's made of."

Billy is on his knees and aiming his shooter at the pot; the guy never uses any spin and he shoots too hard most of the time. Besides, he uses a rug to kneel on and a rabbit's fur under his shooting hand. All these guys are wearing corduroys and they don't wanna dirty 'em. Archie's overalls have holes in the knees and the knuckles on his right hand are scabbed, raw, and bleeding—that's the way to play marbles. He turns to go when something catches his eye.

He can't take his eye off the marble Arnold is spinning into the dirt. It's big and it's pretty, the prettiest shooter he has ever seen. It has all the bright colors and when it's spinning a purple color flashes in and out of sight showing how fast it's spinning. Archie decides that he must have this weapon.

"Hey, Arnold. Ya wanna play for keeps?" The low-key banter ceases and all the boys stand up to stare at the new guy.

Arnold recovers first. "You're too little to play with us. Go home and tell your mama she wants you." Arnold and the crowd laugh at this joke. "And what kinda marbles ya got anyway? Ya probably only got 'dobies and steelies."

"No. I got good marbles. I won 'em fair and square over at Bobby Watson's house."

"Bobby Watson? He would never let a dumb little kid like you come over to his house. And he damn sure ain't gonna letch'ya win his marbles. I oughtta knock your block off for lying."

"I didn't win Bobby's. I won everybody else's though."

Billy says, "Maybe ya oughtta play him, Arnie. Teach him a lesson." Archie sees the big wink Billy throws at his brother.

Arnold walks over to Archie. "You're the dumb kid that's always first in line at the picture show. And ya only brought nine cents last week. I'm surprised they let you outta the house. Let's see your marbles."

"They're at home."

"At home? All that big talk and you ain't got no marbles in your pocket?"

"I can get 'em in a jiffy."

"Well...if you bring back any bad marbles I'm gonna make ya eat 'em."

***

"Dang! That kid's good. Ya see the way he shot those edger shots? Spun his shooter right up into the pot and once he got in there he cleaned out all the dates. Guess he got all your marbles, Arnie." The talker is Curley Malone, a short skinny dark haired kid of thirteen.

Arnold whirls around to face Curley. "Shut up 'afore I bust ya one in the mouth. He ain't no good, just lucky's all. And he ain't leaving here with my marbles in his pocket. Who's gonna grub stake me?"

Tom Bailey, who never says much but packs a big punch in his right fist, says, "Ain't nobody gonna loan you some dates. Your rules, remember?"

"I'll put all the marbles I won up against your shooter."

Arnold's jaw drops as he turns to stare at Archie. "That's my best shooter. You trying to chisel me out of my best shooter? I'll knock you into the middle of next week. I'm not gonna put my best shooter in the pot."

Billy says, "Come on, Arnie. You're a lot better than he is. Put your shooter in there and send the little pissant home crying." Archie sees that wink again.

Archie can't take his eyes off the magnificent shooter setting on a peak in the middle of the ring as he carefully scrapes dirt into peaks with his left hand and places a date on the new peak with his right hand. He counts 150 marbles, all his winnings as he stands up and looks at the biggest pot he has ever seen. This is going to be the best thing he has ever done.

He stands beside Arnold facing the lag line ten yards beyond the other side of the ring. Arnold says, "You go first." Archie lofts his shooter high into the air with lots of spin on it. Then he races around the ring and runs beside the spinning marble as it bounces then rolls to a stop just a whisker from the lag line. He whoops for joy.

"Grab dates!" Archie hears the scream and turns to see Arnold and Billy scrambling on the ground, stirring up a dust storm. They ain't protecting their corduroys no more.

"No fair. No fair."Archie hollers as he races towards the brothers. "This ain't no fair. We was playing a fair and square game."

Arnold stands up and finishes stuffing his pockets with marbles. "Oh yeah? What're ya gonna do about it? Ya wantta fight?"

"You're too big. I just want my marbles back. I won 'em fair and square."

Billy says, "I see Paulie across the street. He'll fight this little snot nose. Hey Paulie, come over here some guy your size is looking for a fight."

Archie recognizes Paulie from school and he knows not even the big guys want to fight him; he's a mean guy. "I don't want to fight nobody. I just want my marbles."

Paulie, his face twisted into a hateful grimace, walks up to Archie and says, "What'sa matter? Yeller?"

Archie don't have time to answer the question, seems like everybody starts shouting, "He's yellow. He's yellow. Let's get him." Archie dodges the first guy and starts running but somebody jumps on his back and rides him to the ground.

Archie's mind leaves him and comes to rest in a tree high above the melee. He sees his body tossed back and forth as five big guys are trying to tear his clothes off. He knows he's twisting, kicking, trying to get loose but he also knows he can't get away. He hears the loud hollering, "Pants him. Let's teach him not to mess with us. Get him good."

Arnold's gloating face comes into focus, and then the smile turns to surprise. Somebody has grabbed Big Arnie by the shirt collar and tosses him aside. "Come on. Be off with ye before I take my belt to the whole lot of ye." The man is old, short, and walks with a bad limp. He's shorter than most of the big boys but he picks them up and throws them aside with ease. When they see the old man's face they run away without a word.

"Come on laddie give me your hand." The guy's smiling as he pulls Archie to his feet. "Don't ya know you can't whip everybody in town? What's your name, boy?"

"Archie Cleebo."

"Your pa Cab Cleebo?" Seeing Archie nod he keeps talking. "I'm Lonnie Johnson. Your dad and me go back a long ways. He ever tell you anything about me?"

"No,"Archie lies. "I know Andy tho'."

"You know old Andy? Hot ziggedy! I got another boy just your size. Maybe you and him can be friends. Come on, let's go over to my house and see if Grandma saved us any dinner."

"What's your other boy's name?"

"Paulie!"

Note   ###

The Archie stories were written for *The Voice* newspaper magazine that was based in the small mining town of Silverton, Idaho. They ran from 2003 through 2006 when the newspaper went out of buisness. The Archie stories are set in the years just prior to WWII and are loosely based on the life of the author.

Archie and his family fled the dust bowl of the Midwest USA and moved to California in 1938 where Ma and Pa Cleebo found harsh conditions and 10 year-old Archie was left largely on his own until he was befriended by neighbors (the Johnsons) with a questionable reputation. Archie, and everyone else, called the matriarch of that family Grandma. Grandma and her family were carnival workers until the carnival folded and then they moved to California where they opened an automobile repair business and thrived until driven out of business by a thug and his influential father.

CASSIOPEIA'S HAIR

by

Nicolas Ridley

Nine tailed fox Tamamo no Mae, under her beautiful human form (down), Utagawa Kuniyoshi

T

he third Tuesday of the month: the book group meeting. Why do I go, Jack? Why do I go? I ask the question but — as with so many questions — I know I should not expect an answer. Jack was a practical man who had no time for fiction.

*

Two bottles of Chardonnay have been drunk. Coffee has been poured for those who drink it; camomile tea for those who don't. Now we have come to that point in the evening when, it might be said, our fate is decided. It is Alison's turn to choose next month's book.

—*Cassiopeia's Hair*, she says.

She holds it up. A frayed, faded, mulberry cover. A dull volume like many others that sit forgotten on the back shelf of a second-hand bookshop. But, as Alison is plainly keen to tell us, the book has a story of its own.—Why I've chosen *Cassiopeia's Hair* is because …

—What is it? asks Barbara. A thriller? A romance? A whodunit?

—I don't know, says Alison.

—Don't know?

—No.

Barbara shakes her head in disbelief.

—Doesn't it say somewhere? asks Cherry.

—No, says Alison.

—Oh.

Cherry allows her eyes to close.

—Who's the author? asks Denise.

—'W', says Alison.

—Who on earth is 'W'?

—That's all it says on the title page. 'W'.

Denise sighs.

There is a pause which I decide I should fill.

—Why have you chosen *Cassiopeia's Hair*, Alison? I ask.

—Well, Elspeth, she says. You remember my Uncle Ivo …

Denise looks at her watch; Cherry leans back on the sofa; *sotto voce* Barbara groans. We've heard the tale before — more than once in fact — but Alison is a dogged storyteller and won't be dissuaded from telling us again. How her Uncle Ivo was found hanging, limp as a soiled overcoat, in a cupboard in a bedroom in the hotel where he was staying in Le *Petit Socco*. How odd it was because Alison has no idea what he was doing in Tangier, having always assumed he seldom strayed far from his lodgings in Broadstairs. How Alison's husband, Gabriel — about whom there will be more later — has a theory. (Alison has always been happy to share Gabriel's theories with anyone who can be persuaded to listen.) Gabriel, it seems, contends that the explanation for Uncle Ivo's death is to be found in the murky world of drug-dealing, money-laundering and espionage. Where Broadstairs fits into this sinister picture I cannot guess, but this seems not to trouble Gabriel.

—So strange, says Alison, placidly. Such a puzzle. Such a mystery ...

Is it? I have no first-hand knowledge of the practice but my reading has ranged widely and — despite my advancing years — I retain most of what I've read. Alison and Gabriel, it seems probable, are unfamiliar with self-induced hypoxia or, as it is often termed, erotic asphyxiation. It is not my intention to enlighten them.

—It was on his bedside table, says Alison.

—I'm sorry ... ?

My attention must have wavered.

—The book. You remember the British Consul arranged for everything they found in Uncle Ivo's hotel room to be shipped back to us. Although Gabriel's quite certain that a number of items haven't been returned and I'm pretty sure that some of the things that were sent back can't possibly have belonged to Uncle Ivo. Anyhow, the book on the bedside table was *Cassiopeia's Hair* and I thought it would be amusing if we read it. It's out of print, of course, but I've done some research on the internet and there are one or two second-hand copies available online.

Barbara, Cherry and Denise have adopted the resigned expression that usually marks this stage of the evening. I should explain that the members of our group have different reading tastes and a book that is chosen by one seldom finds any favour with the rest. The usual practice, however, is to accept what's been proposed as a *fait accompli* and to say nothing further. Which is why Freya's intervention comes as a surprise.

—First, I should tell you that I will be leaving next week and won't be attending any more meetings, she says. Secondly, if you take my advice, you will choose a different book.

—Oh, says Alison.

—Why? says Barbara.

—Have you read *Cassiopeia's Hair?* says Cherry.

—No, says Freya, I haven't read it. But, based on my experience with many other book groups and implausible as it may sound, choosing to read *Cassiopeia's Hair* invariably brings bad luck.

—Bad luck? says Alison.

—Yes, says Freya. Extraordinary misfortune.

There is another pause which this time I decide I will not fill.

—What s- s- superstitious nonsense! says Alison.

She is a stubborn woman who stutters when she's crossed.

—The book I've chosen is *Cassiopeia's Hair,* she says, and that's the book I'd like us all to read.

Freya smiles and says nothing. As she often does, she unfastens the elastic band and writes a word or two in her notebook.

—What do you think, Elspeth? says Denise.

—Me? I say. Oh, I'm happy with whatever you all decide.

My policy is to acquiesce. This is what's expected of a woman of my age.

I joined the book group after Jack died hoping for some intellectual stimulation. A forlorn hope as it happens. By no stretch of the imagination can our discussions be described as 'literary'. The choice of titles is 'eclectic' and see-saws wildly from month to month.

Freya makes another note. What has she seen? What has she heard? What oddity? What idiosyncrasy? A turn of phrase; a sudden colouring; a particular tilt of the head: fragments she will store away for later use. This is her way. The witchcraft of her calling. Freya takes from us what she wants.

My eyes rest on each one of them in turn.

Alison, when she was younger, must have been pretty. Today she has a fondness for lush romances and historical fiction.

Barbara, dark, intense, divorced, is a potter with a studio in an abandoned bakery. She has no sense of humour and favours steam punk and gothic horror.

When the choice of book is Cherry's, she turns to me. Bored, sleepily seductive, she is married to a diver who returns from the oil fields to devote himself to home improvement.

Denise, a science teacher in an all-girls school, claims to have no time for men. In life they have disappointed her but in fiction she is thrilled by the gritty heroes of violent westerns.

And me? As you will guess from my name, I am from a different generation. My choice would always be a novel by the incomparable Mr Charles Dickens — his colourful characters, his well-worked plots — but, whenever I have made the suggestion, there has been a chorus of dissent. (I am considered too old to take offence.) 'Oh, no, Elspeth.' 'Too long.' 'Too boring.' 'Too difficult to follow.' I defer and suggest *Jane Austen*. Together we have read: *Sense and Sensibility, Pride and Prejudice, Mansfield Park, Emma, Northanger Abbey and Persuasion*. We have thus exhausted Miss Austen.

For a time I endeavoured to be more experimental. We tried poetry but it wasn't liked. The stage directions in the play I chose caused confusion. My excursion into erotic fiction was ill-judged. *The English Mistress* turned out to be both poorly written and anatomically improbable. A little mischievously, I then proposed *Mobius the Stripper* by Gabriel Josipovici. I knew, of course, that post-modernism would not be to the group's taste but I knew, also, that the name of its author would be an irresistible attraction.

Is now the time to say more about Alison's husband, Gabriel? 'My Angel Gabriel,' as she likes to call him. No, I think not. Gabriel is at the same time at the centre of this story and at its periphery. But to me he matters very little which is why, when I introduce him, I won't have much to say.

Eventually I conceded defeat. I read my Dickens alone and share my joy in him with no one else. When the choice of book is mine, or when Cherry shrugs and looks in my direction, I settle for a detective novel. Nothing 'noir', you understand. At this stage of my life I have no need of 'noir'. The country house, the castle, the isolated vicarage, the lonely hotel. These are my preferred settings. And, of course, the eccentric detective who, at the close, correctly identifies the least likely suspect as the villain of the piece. Such books are, I believe, what keeps our group together. We share the pleasure of a conclusion, a resolution with no loose ends. To me it seems not unreasonable to expect to read a final sentence and find that everything has been explained. When all is said and done, life is puzzling enough; I see no need for fiction to add to the confusion.

—Is this simplistic of me? I once asked Freya, as we sat, drinking coffee, in 'The Bottomless Cup'.

—No, I don't think so, she said. A writer may pose as many questions as she likes but there should be answers.

—And if the reader fails to find them?

—There are always readers who can contrive to lose themselves in their own back gardens.

*

The clue was obvious: the notebook fastened with a rubber band. That and the way she watched us, the way she listened.

—Forgive me, I said, touching her arm. I would like to ask you a question.

The meeting — the first Freya attended — had come to a close and we were standing in the street.

—You may ask, she said, but I may choose not to answer.

—Am I right in thinking that you are a novelist?

I saw the lie she considered telling me floating between us like a bubble. And then it burst.

—Yes. Although I'd be grateful if you said nothing to anyone else.

—Of course. I'm noted for my discretion.

—It can provoke such tiresome questions.

—I understand, I said.

—Yes, she said. I think you do.

And trust was established between us.

The next Thursday we met for coffee and for many Thursdays after that. I learn that Freya — writing under a name I won't divulge — publishes a novel every other year and has done all her writing life. Her practice, while she is working on her first and second drafts, is to live away from home, isolated from all distractions. Does she have a husband? Or children? Friends who miss her? Celebrations she can't attend? She shared none of this with me.

—Writing is lonely business, she told me one afternoon. But it's what I do.

—Is that why you joined the book club? I said. For company?

—Partly. And also for the remarkable characters I come across.

—Indeed?

I ponder this. Alison? Brenda? Cherry? Denise? (Should I explain what must surely be obvious? The alphabetical names I have ascribed to my fellow members are entirely fictional. I am, as I say, noted for my discretion.) It must be, I suppose, a part of the novelist's craft to discover what others miss, or otherwise to find what isn't there at all. Should she also be expected to uncover the narrative that lies behind the characters? No, that must be the preserve of the clairvoyant. At the time there was no story. Only the circumstances that would lead to one.

*

Jack and I shared an interest in brainteasers; casse-têtes my husband used to call them. He regarded such exercises as mental gymnastics and thus as acceptable as calisthenics.

Are you acquainted with the puzzle of the black and white hats? There are, of course, different versions but this is mine.

Three women line up on a staircase. Standing one behind the other, they face in the same direction. The women are wearing hats which they have taken from a closet in an unlit room. None of them knows the colour of the hat she is wearing but they have been told that there were in the closet three black hats and two white hats.

The woman on the top stair can see the colour of the hats worn by the women on the middle and bottom stairs. The woman on the middle stair can see the hat worn by the woman below her on the bottom stair but not the hat worn by the woman behind her on the top stair. The woman on the bottom stair cannot see the colour of the hats worn by the women behind her. The woman on the top stair is asked the question:

—Do you know what colour your hat is?

She thinks for a moment.

—No, she says. I don't.

The woman on the middle stair is asked the same question:

—Do you know what colour your hat is?

She, too, thinks for a moment

—No, she says. I don't.

The woman on the bottom stair is then asked the question …

—Well, she says, if neither the woman on the top stair nor the woman on the middle stair knows what colour her hat is, then, yes, by deduction, I know the colour of *my* hat. It is …

I will not pretend this is an analogy or a metaphor or anything such as that. I am not a novelist. Such devices aren't my stock in trade. All I will say is that whenever I bring to mind Alison, Brenda, Cherry and Denise — and, of course, Gabriel — I am reminded of the puzzle of the black and white hats.

*

The last afternoon I will spend with Freya. I am going to miss her presence at the book group. To employ a weary cliché — permissible only because, before her arrival, I felt so suffocated — she has been 'a breath of fresh air'. When invited to contribute to the discussion, she has led us away from the trivial, anecdotal and banal. However dreary the subject under discussion, her comments have been concise, illuminating, well-considered. I find myself — a sign of frailty — on the point of asking her if she cannot stay a little longer. A foolish impulse. Everything must come to an end. Few people know this better than I.

—Tell me, I say. I'm intrigued. Were you serious when you said we shouldn't read *Cassiopeia's Hair?*

Freya looks at me.

—Oh, yes, she says. Entirely serious. Over the years, I've attended several book groups that have chosen it. Terrible disasters always follow. Please don't ask me for an explanation. I can't provide one.

—How very strange.

—Extraordinary, isn't it?

And now we are standing on the pavement outside 'The Bottomless Cup'.

—Goodbye, I say. I'll miss our Thursday coffees.

—Yes, she says. So will I. Goodbye.

—I don't suppose we'll meet again, will we?

—No, I don't suppose we will.

—May I give you my address, I say. In case you should ever wish to get in touch.

—Thank you, she says, and accepts the card I give her.

*

It's time to speak of Gabriel. Jack would have called him 'one of those pretty boys'. I would describe him as 'charming'. In my experience, 'charm' is not a serious attribute and most of those who are 'blessed' with charm use it recklessly. I feel the need to say nothing more about Gabriel.

*

I won't dress up the facts. I will lay them out as clinically as I can. Like a frog on a dissecting table; at the same time pitiable and repellent. But it was nothing as simple as a love triangle.

Alison likes to show me her wedding photographs. Alison and Gabriel: the glowing bride in white; the bridegroom's boyish grin. But later — very soon — Brenda appears in the shadows. A burning passion, Brenda tells me. Uncontrollable. Her affair with Gabriel is a poorly-kept secret although Alison herself suspects nothing. At different times Cherry and Denise share with me their surprise that anyone could be so blind. But Brenda, too, is blind. While her husband is in the oil fields, Cherry finds herself lonely. Gabriel, she says, is such lovely company. Denise, brooding darkly, dismisses them all. They cannot reach into his soul, she tells me. They cannot bring him happiness. Some day. When the time is right. She pours herself another glass of wine and stares ahead into a future which she will share with Gabriel once she has sprung him free.

How do I know this? I have found myself their regular confessor. Discretion and indifference are readily confused.

*

The boil swells. And then it bursts.

The details are the trivial currency of domestic drama. A husband who does not return from a sales conference. An unexplained voicemail message. An undeleted text. An old restaurant bill in a jacket pocket. A hotel key hidden in a drawer. So tedious. So banal. One thing which leads to another and another and another. Deceits unravelling. Denials and confessions. Fury and tears. Alison confronts Brenda. Together they rage at Cherry. Denise unleashes her pent-up scorn on them all. Such treachery. Such vitriol. Nothing can ever be forgiven.

Gabriel remains absent for several days but in due course he will be found and everything will be explained.

*

No. I don't miss the book group. If Freya hadn't joined it when she did, I would have left the four of them to snipe and bicker without me. And, no, I've not read *Cassiopeia's Hair* and I think it unlikely that I will.

*

Henrietta — we learn later — is a young woman in the Accounts Department: an ordinary-looking girl, who has never before been the object of office gossip. A puzzle. But sexual chemistry is often a mystery. For the present, she and Gabriel live contentedly in a terraced house. On clear nights they take a telescope into the back garden and stand there together watching the stars

*

Sometimes — often unexpectedly — Jack answers me. There are things, he says, we can easily explain. There are things we can explain less easily. There are also things that it may sometimes seem we cannot explain at all. But this is not to say they cannot be explained. Only that we cannot explain them. Everything has its explanation, says Jack, although some explanations are hidden from us. Jack was a practical man who had no time for fiction.

*

The envelope is addressed to me. Bold handwriting that I do not recognise. Inside is a postcard — a reproduction of *The Death of Chatterton* by Henry Wallis — and a short, typewritten note:

My dear E.

I feel the need to confess. As you will know, a novelist's task and aspiration is to persuade the reader that her narrative is true. Trust me, she says. I won't deceive you. But fiction is, of course, a lie. A lie that we — the reader and the writer — conspire together to believe. However, in the present case, the lie was more in the nature of a deceit. To put it plainly: I have had no previous experience of book groups. Joining one was an experiment, a piece of research. I knew and know nothing about the book that was found on Uncle Ivo's bedside table in his hotel in Le Petit Socco. Reading Cassiopeia's Hair — indeed merely mentioning its name — may bring bad luck but it doesn't seem very likely, doesn't it? My story was an invention. It is what I do.

Forgive me.

F.

###

For Old Times' Sake

by

Billy O'Callaghan

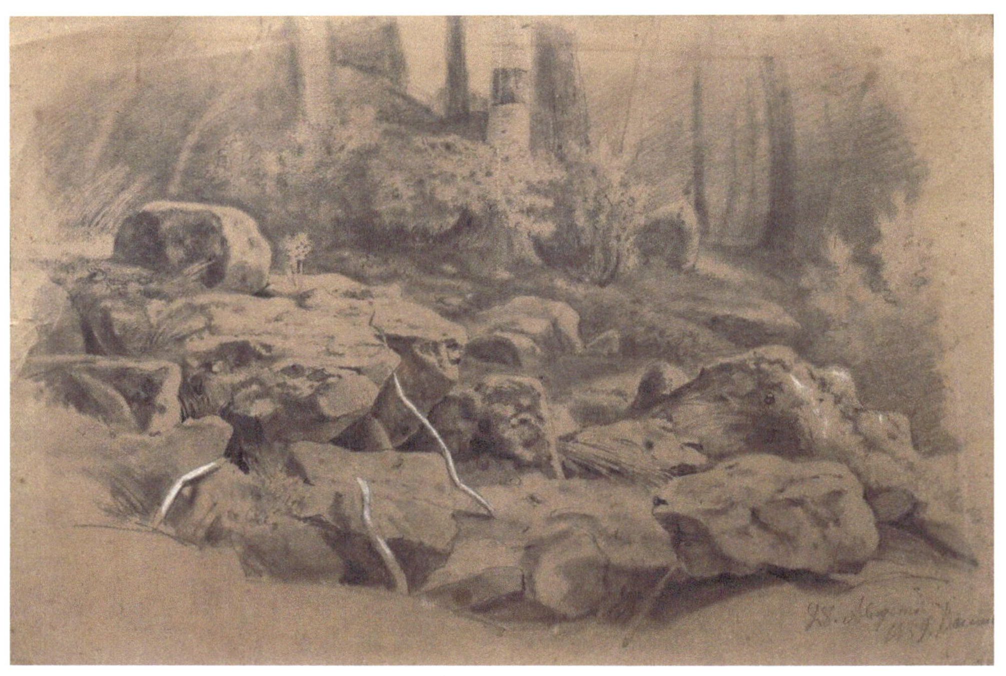

Stones by Ivan Shishkin

I am sitting at my father's table, going through his personal effects, when his address book falls open onto the floor. Glad of this distraction, I pick it up and begin scanning the list of names.

Lydia Barstow is on the second page, the third entry under 'B'.

Christ, the past is always there, waiting. In a heartbeat I am a boy again, thirteen years old, doing what boys do. The light on, the curtains split just wide enough to see. And me, tucked away behind my window, with pennies for eyes, watching. Looking back, she must have known I was there, but if she did then she never let on. Maybe she even got something out of it. We all have needs as well as wants.

Actually calling her up is a throwaway notion, but the problem is that nothing looks quite itself at dusk.

Twilight has a peculiar way of condensing everything, real and unreal alike.

She picks up on the second ring, as if she has been waiting all this time, forty some-odd years, for the call, expecting it. Impossible, of course, but that's how it feels. There is that lovely claxon sound as I pluck out the numbers on the old-fashioned dial, followed by a bar and a half of robotic chirping as a code builds and breaks itself open. And then, into a cough of emptiness, a sultry, questioning "Hello?"

For a moment, my mind flushes with all sorts of things and all sorts of nothing.

"Uh, hi. Could I speak with Lydia, please? Oh, it is? Lydia Barstow?"

Well, Lydia Barstow that was. Lydia Hunsecker now, and for about as long as the road to hell and back, but yeah, Barstow, too, she guesses, once upon a time anyway. But why, and who's asking?

"This is Steve Glick, I don't suppose you remember me. From next door, back when... Yes, in Laurens. That's right, little Stevie Glick. Except not so little anymore... Changed? Well, I... It's been a long time. No, no, not anymore, not for years now. That's all cleared up. What? Oh right, yes. Thank God. Kenny? My brother, Kenny? He's fine. Well, I say fine. He lives up in Oregon now. In a log cabin way the hell out in the ass-end of beyond. You believe that? Well yeah, I guess he was always a bit wild. He's retired, of course, that's right, a teacher, yes, and these days he's into this whole hippy trip that he missed out on first time round. Got himself a beard down to here and a wife who's not even half his age and who goes around braless and barefoot seven months of the year. He's happy, though, which is what counts. What's that? You did? Really? Wait 'til I tell him, he'll be tickled purple. But I suppose he did have his moments. Let me guess. The curls, right? Those curls did it for a lot of girls, back in the day. No, no. Long gone, I'm afraid. Sorry. What? Oh that. No, he is fine. I just meant about him losing an arm. You knew about that, didn't you? Oh, he's right as spring rain now. It was all a long time ago. I guess I just assumed you knew. He always says how lucky he was to have made it back at all. Christ, we all were. A pisser, indeed. That's a word for it, all right. A hell of a word for it. Yeah, I will. Sure I will."

Lydia Barstow, after decades of existing only as wrought-iron dreams, suddenly alive and real again, and hard and hungry as the tip of a pick hacking at the wood of my inner ear.

A lot has changed, of course. Passing years have tagged the once-pure soprano lilt of her voice with a textured addendum that evokes little cool finger snaps or pages on the verge of crumbling, and her background breath has the bobbing inconsistency of a chimney breeze. But still, my mind insists on picturing her as she once was. Forever seventeen, timeless in the manner of standing stones. The senses work of their own accord, I suppose, but I can't shake the notion that somehow, through a series of spun numbers, I have found a way of quantum leaping. I'm talking witchery of a high degree here, magic that would have made the ancients come apart in hosannas of madness. In our airy small-talk way we find ourselves traversing not merely miles in their thousands but time in its decades' worth. Telephones play such wicked tricks. In a single sleight-of-hand, I have exhumed and reawakened the dead-and-buried past of 1961. My past, full of sweetness and glory and even back then probably nine-tenths imagined.

"Listen," I say, urgency hook-punching holes in the walls of my throat. "The reason I'm calling is because I feel like a thank-you is in order. In fact, it's long overdue. Christ, I thought I could just choke this out and then that'd be it and you'd either take umbrage and hang up with a bang or else you'd find a funny side to it and we'd maybe even end up raising a few giggles. But suddenly all my best intentions seem to have gotten stuck somewhere in the back of my head. Well, all right. Deep breath and here goes. It will probably seem a bit silly to you, and actually I'm kind of hoping it will, but I just want to say thanks, you know, thanks a lot, for leaving your curtains open just enough..."

For some interminable length of time I am left to sit here, empty as a pot and feeling a little bit like the Coyote in those Road Runner cartoons, that wily old ever-optimistic fool hunched over behind some rock with his eyes squeezed shut and his fingers jammed in his ears to at least the second knuckle, waiting for the special ACME mail-order rocket-bomb to work the way it is designed to instead of the way it will. Then, finally, a little breathy laughter breaks the emptiness, rattling like a penny in a tin box from a two-pack a day habit, two packs at least, and the need for words becomes redundant.

In 1961 I was thirteen years old, and knew all there was to know about the things that seem important only until your hormones take flame and fire the world into an entirely different colour. My formal education was a shoplifted and well-thumbed copy of Playboy that I'd procured from Timmy Swanson for the princely sum of two rather peachy forty-fives, Chuck Berry's 'Too Pooped To Pop' and Sam Cooke's 'Twistin' The Night Away', records that had become mine by virtue of some hand-me-down inheritance law after my brother, Kenny, fell into his dyed-in-red-fur folkie phase. Timmy was a neighbourhood kid and not really a friend of mine. He had a year on me in school and even back then you could feel the inevitability of some serious jail-time glooming up his horizon. But that extra year counted. Playboy was already just a shrug of the shoulders to him, no biggie, but blues and soul had become a kind of holy grail, especially since his father kept a special spastic-level of rage set aside for so-called 'coloured' music. Deke Swanson was a fair-to-middling ex-bruiser who spent big hours working his way up the rankings as a heavyweight drunk, and nothing in this world or any other could light his fuse like the holler of a black man on the radio. Timmy seemed to pleasure in cranking his old man's gears and often came to school wearing the results of those rages like Purple Hearts, but in those days people, even teachers, could still look and look away from that sort of business. The way they viewed it, kids were forever stepping out of line and the occasional upside tap was simply the world's way of packing them back in their box.

Trading with Timmy did push me forward on the page, but I was still wrestling strictly within two dimensions and had yet to find a way of successfully turning paper into flesh. For that I needed a mentor, one who not only knew the ropes but also how to play them. Step forward the lovely Lydia.

Back then, she'd been middle teens at a hard push, but already she had a Sandra Dee thing going on. She was a bonfire in a storm, blonde-bobbed and bubbly as shaken soda, with big cerulean eyes that shifted shade as the day juggled its light and the kind of permanent top-to-bottom smile that could have breathed life back into a blackened blood cell. She was firecrackers and dark ponds, burning you up and then numbing you to a standstill; she was space candy on the tongue, that alive. Cut, admittedly, from that well-visited and by then already-starting-to-bedraggle Marilyn cloth but still not a wannabe, at least not in any kind of pathetic way. And all she had going and all she'd ever have was put on nightly display just a house's distance away from mine, the whole beautiful array within easy reach of a well-trained eye.

Nights summer and winter would find me huddled at my window in the darkness, armed with the set of binoculars that my father had hauled through the wringers of Guadalcanal, Peleliu and Okinawa. Eventually, often after a wait that would have strung my resolve to an inch past snapping, she'd appear, delicately prancing back and forth between a wardrobe and her bed, her room backlit like a Vegas stage, her body slim as a sapling fir and loose-limbed as any dancer. On a good night I'd happen across her in her skinnies, and you could actually feel the screams of the world's breaks as they struggled against gravity's turn, desperate to make a mountain out of a moment. But on the best nights, the very best, when the stars fell into rare alignment and the elements were all in balance, I'd catch her wearing nothing at all. By some holy and magical conjunction, every dream that had ever bucked a kick inside my head came breathlessly true, and that was me, done for, boned and rolled, my limbs turned cobweb, my mind reduced to a useless, quivering mess. She was a mortal lock for stunning; cute as one of those red-assed bumblebees and sweet as ballpark pickle.

Try to understand just what kind of animal the average thirteen-year-old 1961-era boy was, with the world finally opening up like a flower for him. You had Elvis doing his thing and Marilyn doing hers. Kennedy was in the White House and drainpipe was the new hip. I was a kid fringing on adolescence, and driven by curiosity, not perversion. And Lydia was my teacher, not really all that different from, say, Mrs. Hennessy, my science teacher, or Miss Barker who taught me History. Well, not all that different. In moving back and forth past the window, clad in underwear or even less, her attention fixed on folding some flimsy blouse or with a poetry book heart-unfurled in one raised hand, Lydia was actually lecturing me on the way of things, just as Smell-the-Cheese Hennessy or Bitch Barker did on the chemical elements or the Battle of Ticonderoga. She was educating me, and education is a gift. How can I be anything but grateful for that?

"I always knew you were watching," she says, and isn't it funny how a smile can make its way into words, how it can physically or chemically change their balance? A little bending seems to lighten them, to turn them easy somehow.

I let the wind escape me, in a silent way, and smile back.

"I sort of guessed you did," I answer. "I mean, nobody gets that lucky that often, do they?"

A curtain has gone up somewhere, revealing the Great and Powerful for who and what she really is. This is a different kind of nakedness, like a wide open embrace. And we have at it, talking about little things, shooting the breeze. I lead, less by choice than by mutual consent, dance-floor rules, the proper thing to do, us being of an age where chivalry can still count as something other than sexist, and I spill the guts of my life only to find the contents merely so-so, with the colours strangely lacking. Not bad, handclaps rather than dynamite blasts, but dull. Marriage: tick; children: tick; nice home, half-decent job, car that looks fine in the driveway and does its duty out on the road. Et cetera, et cetera. Honest answers, but suddenly, distilled to this, devastating in their emptiness. It is some wake-up call. For years, decades, we live these lives that seem okay, but the fulcrum in that statement is the lagging verb, and to create the illusion of balance we cling to the only survival mechanism available to us: myth. The myth that we are doing enough, as if getting by is all that matters. I say my piece, without once stumbling onto a single worthwhile subject, then gust out a lungful of sigh and unfurl an ellipsis that cedes to her the ground and everything on it.

She enters the limelight a star in the making. The contrast between us is like Kansas and Oz. What she has to say is hardly the stuff of Arabian nights, but she navigates the various twists and turns with an ease worth envying. She'd married out of college, after less than six weeks of courtship. A big fucking mistake. Fucking, delivered in the loose-handed way of poets grown soul-weary from seeing their hopes so continuously torched. Officially of old-woman age, but really getting her gusto blowing, putting her shoulder into it.

Hubby was Felix Hunsecker, a travelling salesman from Bowling Green, Ohio, thirteen years her senior and the type who believed everything he uttered was a commandment dictated from on high. He was her cross to bear, and the biggest of all her many mistakes was buying so recklessly into all that sanctity-of-marriage bullshit. Because she'd have thrived in Paris, or New York. But getting free was the thing. Still is, actually. Felix has been dead a tad over two years now, and she is still unearthing little snarls of him around the house. A handkerchief here, a balled-up sock there, the diamond tongue of a necktie jammed in mid-pant by some carelessly shut bureau drawer. Plus, he'd had this fixation on writing notes, got through roughly a post-it pad a month. Two years on, those little yellow bastards continue to pop up, flapping on some draught and almost always stating the fucking obvious. If the clock stops, it probably needs winding. At the beginning, when she was still young and gullible enough to be blinded by the lightning notion that some man might actually want to put up with her for more than five minutes, such compulsive scribbling had seemed cute, even the pearls of incessantly moronic wisdom. But that cuteness grew warts in a hurry.

"You know, Stevie, at first I thought it was your father watching me. But that didn't fit the profile. He was too grown up for such nonsense, and too far away. If you know what I mean. And with me, he was always the perfect gentleman. I think he did like me, though. Not in that way, but maybe I reminded him of somebody he'd once known, some girl who'd danced off with a little piece of him, a piece he'd never been able to properly replace. That happens, you know. That's where the hollowness comes from. I remember him on the porch of an evening, sitting there sucking on that old Popeye pipe. It seems funny putting this out there now, but he was my first crush. With the likes of your father around, Tyrone Power's job was safe as the lock on Fort Knox's front door, but handsome isn't everything, is it? He was always too thin, and he had this nervous, bowlegged walk that you only get if the Lord's really itching for you, but his smile was just the ticket. Well, I guess I don't have to tell you."

She is right about the smile. It ran clean through, like wood grain. Despite all that he'd seen and known, my father was a man made of gentle things.

I feel embarrassed but not surprised at finding myself close to tears. The funeral has been done to dust but, even a month on, certain details still feel close enough to touch. I clear my throat and explain to Lydia that I am really just calling on a whim, having discovered her number in an old address book. It's fallen on me to clear out the old man's belongings, his personal effects. Kenny would have come, but Oregon is so far removed. Since packing in Des Moines, My wife and I live in East Peru, must be getting on for seventeen years now, and my Chevy can haul me from our front door to the Laurens town limits inside of three hours. Faster, if I feel like gunning a death rattle out of the old girl.

We hold a few breaths of stillness, Lydia slightly throaty at her end, set to tingling by some shadowy thing that has taken hold and is not for letting go, and I numb to the marrow at mine, raked out in a way that needs no explanation. You step back far enough, grief softens to fog, and the world remains real but not all the way real. But the crux of what I have just said hangs between us, and we both catch a draught of it. The fact that my father had stowed her contact details through all these years, even if he had never actually bothered to get in touch, barks with implied significance.

"He was my first crush," she says again, and her voice flutters with a kind of giggle and turns tender, wistful. "I pined away nights beyond counting, the way all girls do when they set their hearts on something unreachable. But looking back, I am glad beyond belief that it was so strictly one-way. Because think of how tainted my memories would have been. Think of the damage it would have caused me."

And after a while, she says, once it became clear to her that she was simply wasting buckshot, she looked around and fixed her eye on my brother. Ken was boyish in a way that could have passed for handsome on a good day, which seemed like most days back then. But he also had something of my father's quietness about him. In the big bad world that didn't count for a whole lot but up on a movie screen it would have been the real deal, shoot-'em-up stuff. Looks go, but character is like the marks a chisel leaves in granite, and that's what keeps the good ones in work long after the pretty boys have passed their sell-by dates.

"That's what I liked most about Kenny. That quietness. It gave him an air of knowing himself, of understanding exactly who he was and who he'd become. So few people have that. He was skinny as a corn shoot and his hair was always too long and too tossed and if he wasn't swinging a baseball bat at thin air then he probably wasn't at least three-quarters the way awake. But a searching eye comes up with its own definition of what's golden. Of course, nothing came of my efforts, not so much as a handshake, but for a while it was pretty nice to dream."

She laughs, and her breath rustles across thousands of miles of telephone line. I lean in and believe that I can almost feel that breath against my cheek.

"I know, I know. I picked the wrong Glick. Story of my life. And you were so much younger than me. Three, four years, was it? When we were kids that made us practically different species. But who can say what might have happened if I'd stuck around a little longer than I had. I always knew you watched me, though, and I guess if I'm totally square about it I must admit to being more than a little flattered. Something about the men in your family always just seemed to rub me right."

My throat aches in that way it does when we need to cry. And yet, the phone has become a kind of tether to the world and I understand that the moment I drop the receiver back into its cradle the stillness will sweep in from all sides. Being alone in this house suddenly feels too much for me and even though it hurts to talk I know it will hurt worse not to, so I keep going, on and on. I recall things, unexpected flashbacks. My father loved baseball and thought nothing of two or three hundred mile round-trips, sometimes with Kenny sprawled out in the back but always with me up front, just to catch one of the big boys, Mantle, Mays, Clemente, Hank Aaron, or so that I could share in the tail-end of old timers like Ted Williams. Guys with the stuff, as he used to say. Even from a young age, I got that it was more than just the game itself he'd been chasing. To him, baseball was about something. The scores and the strikes mattered, but they were never what mattered most.

I had friends when I was a kid, though not many and none that were truly close. My nature, I think, tended toward introversion. I'd been turned wrong from reading and as a result thought too deeply about things and the consequences of things. Where secrets were concerned, my head was an Alcatraz, and in this way, and in some other ways too, I was far more like my father than Kenny was. Lydia missed that, I guess because of the age difference between us, but I'm sure that even if she'd taken the time to look she still wouldn't have seen. Things can be real and yet intangible, and you either know and recognise them for what they are or else you miss them entirely as they pass you by.

My father was a quiet man, and as deep in his way as any ocean. But there were moments when the wind changed that he'd talk to beat the band. And it's all here, in my head and, I suppose, my heart, every wise and foolish thing he ever said to me. Because, right or not, it was stuff that worked. I loved him, of course, and I loved to listen while he talked. He knew the names of all the trees and birds in our neck of the proverbial, and could hit precisely on just what it was that had made DiMaggio so much a man in such a game of boys. And sometimes, when his mood turned just so, he'd even start in about the war. A little of the way in, at least, up to his shins, just talking but from out of his own depths and with an oddly stoic kind of violence.

I was always the prompt. Looking for a tree to climb or a dragonfly to snag, I'd plug gaps with a turn at the punch-line scene of some John Wayne shoot-'em-up. I had the swagger down pat, too: a way of rolling my shoulders and a certain affected pelvic drag, and even if my Now just a darn minute, Pilgrim, catchphrase happened to fall an inflection or two shy of the ideal then it was still close enough for comfort.

My father would sit there, raking the prong of some stick idly through the embers of our campfire, and chuckle without needing to look up. Most of the time he'd let it go, but occasionally something about it would catch him like a briar snarling wool and he'd clear his throat and say no, sorry Stevie but no, John Wayne and all of those Hollywood big shots were selling it wrong, because war was nothing like the movies. What it mostly was, he said, was being afraid, even during the long stretches of boredom when you'd almost find yourself wishing for a little action, and what terrified you most was not even the idea of dying as much as the thought that maybe you wouldn't be able to measure up. That when the moment arrived you'd be too numb to move. Every soldier sets out lopsided with thoughts of heroism, he said, but he'd been through the thick end of it and had seen and done enough to know that Sherman, for all his bullshit and bravado, really had nailed the whole sordid business to a tree. War truly is hell, black as night and smoking hot.

"Think about that," he said, and I waited the requisite moment, then nodded and said I would. The way we all do when a thing is easy to say.

This call feels like my old man's parting gift. Lydia listens, laughs, and now and again skirts against a place of tears. We talk, the way people do when they are trying to grope their way through a downpour of sudden, unexpected grief, and it feels genuine, I think on both ends. With night coming in, my childhood feels like a blush of winter sledding and summer days spent hiking out in the woods or fishing for steelies up at Pickerel Lake. It feels real, a thing that actually did happen and was not simply imagined, a thing that will leave a small but indelible mark on the roll of time. And there is reassurance to be had from that.

When I finally run out of juice, the better part of an hour has been lost. Evening is about to give out, and the last of a soft October sunlight hangs in blood-orange spatters across one pink-papered wall. I have reminisced myself hoarse and laugh a little at how unlike me it is to be so open. Lydia catches my laughter but reads it wrong, mistakenly deciphers an unwritten word for panic in amongst the mix, and asks, with genuine concern, whether or not I have anyone here with me tonight. I say no, I have the lane all to myself and am rolling this one alone.

The fact that tonight will likely be the last I ever spend in this house is one I leave unsaid. In many ways, the miscellaneous details that need tending to around here are a pretence, or an excuse.

"I am fine on my own," I say, which is mostly true. But more than that, more than anything, it is how I want it.

Elspeth, my wife, had offered to travel up with me, but her arthritis has recently been pinching something rotten and I latched onto that as an excuse to lay down a little law and to tell her no, thanks but no, that what she needed to do was sit back and get her feet up, take it easy. Lengthy jaunts in the car are the stuff of axe-murders on her in that state. And, thankfully, Elspeth is one of those women who get the hook of a cryptic crossword. If a story has nothing going on between its lines then it holds no appeal whatsoever for her. Out of duty, she'd pulled an inevitably disagreeable face, but finally nodded to my demands and let me kiss her. Still able to pucker with the best of them, and still as always nailing me down to my boot heels.

"But don't you find it strange?" Lydia says against my ear. "To find the place so empty, I mean?"

I purse my mouth and admit that I do, at least a little. This was a house built with life in mind, and emptiness is not at all its natural state. I laugh again, wanting to set things at ease, but the sound echoes all around me and feels uncertain in the room. Lydia tries to laugh too, but the line does not translate the gesture too well and after a second or two she kills it with the suggestion that if I should find myself struggling to sleep then I absolutely must call her up again, time be damned. Hardly cracking a dream anymore is, in her considered opinion, one of the truly great ass-aches of old age, that and all the bran you need to chow if you have any interest at all in keeping even semi-regular. But she has enjoyed the call, and the chance to dig up a few old bones.

"Don't hesitate," she says. "Now that you know the number, use it. I'll be bunking down for the foreseeable with a big fat Updike, so you can count on me being wide awake. The toothpicks are already in place. Three, four in the AM: it's all the same to me. Clocks hold no authority around here, anymore. So just dial, okay?"

A goodbye silence presses in. Static bleeds into the line in tiny, shapeless whispers, imprints of things long since said and done, breaths spent like easy money. Unable to think of anything further to add, I thank her once more, a composite thank you blanket-embracing all I'd already said and all I'd been hoping to say but hadn't quite found the way. She reiterates her invitation to call, insisting that I no longer have any reason now to be shy.

"And if you really can't sleep," she adds, her voice all the way seventeen again and soft as birdsong, "why not try looking out your window?" Tossed into the pot as a parting joke, but perhaps meant as some small thing more, a kind of permission as well as an offer of forgiveness. I hang up on a thin so-long but linger at the table, until the hour grows late and a plummy darkness has thickened the entire immediate world to mud. Then I surrender.

By four or so, I am done with even trying to sleep. At my age, you understand that there are nights when sleep comes and nights when it is somewhere else, a long way off from you. My old bed feels damp in that way beds do when they have not been slept in for a long time. The sheets are clean but clammy, and the pillow still and unyielding, no longer used to a steady flow of dreams.

I lie here, playing dead, moved only by shallow breath, feeling my age but also feeling absurdly young. My life as I once upon a time lived it hangs within touching distance. Even the air tastes of it. With a cough of sadness I realise just how many hopeful thoughts I have left behind in this room, good solid longings simply abandoned. The places I intended visiting, the millions I'd make, the girls I was going to kiss, consequences be damned, starting of course with Lydia Barstow. And when I can bear these thoughts no longer, I rise and dress quickly, go downstairs, put on a pot of strong coffee and set to work.

Amid a clutter of tacky little carnival souvenirs and age-browned paperbacks that stir awake long-forgotten and most unexpected joys, the occasional photograph passes through my hands, of my father and mother young and laughing, looking too mighty, too immense for the trap of black and white. But I refuse to dwell on any one detail. Drawers and wardrobes need stripping, boxes wait to be filled.

And on towards dawn, when I hear a movement over near the foot of the stairs, an echo that has all the reedy vibrations of a father calling for a son to get up, the fish are waiting but won't wait forever, I sigh the sound away as nothing more than the rattle of heating pipes in the wall. All words echo. Every footstep leaves a mark, however vague. I seal up one box and, without even checking my pace, start straight in on the next.

###

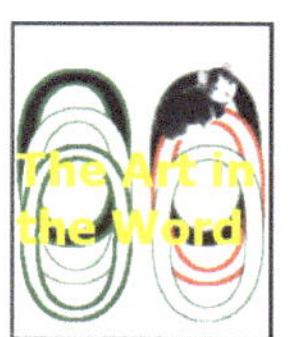

The Art in
the Word